About Rushati Ghosh

Rushati Ghosh has been secretly writing stories since early childhood days, hiding them under table mats, bed mattresses and in her brother's retired toy boxes. She is also a book hoarder and dreams of owning a Library of her own. Apart from a well-travelled passport, she holds multiple library cards and practises the art of teleportation. And now that she has visited multiple parallel worlds, she needs to tell the world about them.

After her wonderful career graph at McKinsey & Co., she has taken a U-turn to enter that realm of creativity where all her characters have waited for long to be introduced to the world.

The Turbo Gang: Inception
Rushati Ghosh

The Turbo Gang: Inception

Rushati Ghosh

Kalamos Literary Services LLP

Kalamos Literary Services LLP
Email: info@kalamos.co.in | editorial@kalamos.co.in
First Published in 2018
by
Kalamos Literary Services
ISBN- 978-93-87780-08-8

The Turbo Gang
Rushati Ghosh

Cover designed and typeset in Kalamos Literary Services LLP
Print and bound in India.

I love the weirdos.

The rule breakers. The strange whimsical,
outlandish, peculiar, and uncanny. The
misfits. The curious, unusual, eccentric, and
unpredictable. The freaks. The radical,
star gazing vagabonds. The loners.
The rejects. The outsiders.
The silly romanticists
who ridiculiously dream
of changing the
world someday...
because they do.

- **Creig Crippen**

To Amritanshu, the weirdo in my life.

Acknowledgements

A big *thank you....*

To my very creative publisher, Anuj Kumar, for his relentless enthusiasm and round-the-clock guidance. To my illustrator, Vibha Sharma, for bringing the story to life. To my editor, Kritika Sharma, for her helpful suggestions.

To my wonderful parents, for introducing me to beautiful stories of courage and wisdom, and a huge bonus collection of books since very early. Thank you for telling me to go beyond the ordinary and tap into my unlimited potential. I am forever indebted. To my stellar brother, Amritanshu, for sharing my dreams, chalking out the possibilities, and kicking hard my creative cells to achieve them, literally. To my perfect better half, Sumeet, for sharing his life, wise words, spells of encouragement and just everything to make me chase my dreams. I couldn't have chosen a better person to share my life with.

And, to my terrific girl gang - Karuna, Bhumika, Swati, for always being there. Always.

Blessed to have you all in my life!

Table of Contents

BEWARE!
THIS BOOK ISN'T SAFE

**If you are looking for
a safe adventure,
this book is not for you.**

**This book might give you
some whacky ideas.
Turn further at your own risk.**

THE iNGLORIOUS MEETING WiTH THE PRiNCiPAL

'Captain America' the leader with a shield, 'Hulk' a big green dude with anger issues, 'Iron Man' with his hi-tech Jarvis and a suit, 'Thor' with a hammer and of course being literally a God etc., etc., etc. Yes, I am talking about none other than 'The Avengers'. But... even they have parents!

Ever imagined what would happen to the world if all the Avengers were sent off to different planets by their parents. The world would come to an end, and there would be chaos everywhere.

Well, that's what happened with us. No, the world, in general, was all fine and there was no chaos anywhere. Except in our lives.

I, and my soul friends, Mikka and Tara, were all leading a happy life in St. Xavier's School for Special Children. To clear the air, there was no 'Professor X' and his X-men. But mutants - kind of yes. For it was us an odd bunch of kids with special needs. Our teachers called us kids with 'super capabilities', but I often wondered about the 'super capabilities' part. Our senior, Rohan Mehta, who is visually impaired, had named our miscreation as 'Mutation' in his farewell speech. The word long passed on to junior batches, and we've called ourselves 'Mutants' since then.

So hi, I am Bikram Bakshi, accidentally nicknamed Bankoo by my parents. (Yes, in the era of Yuvi-s and Adi-s, that, unfortunately, is my nickname.) My mutation is that I don't walk, I wheel.

Anyway, getting back to how it all started, the big bang, the origin, the inception. Well, as it turned out, one day our parents, these arch-enemies we were born with, decided it was time for us to leave our beloved Special School and instead, go to a regular school.

Our parents were called in turns by the principal ma'am, Mrs. Srivastava, in her office on Saturday. It was PTM Day, one of those days that haunt almost all of us long before and after the meet. I didn't know it disturbed quite many parents as well. Mom wore a really dull sari that day with very light lipstick. Not that she was trying to carry a nude look. Just that she was preparing herself to attend a very sad and agonizing event of her life, all thanks to me. She didn't talk to me at all the previous day and night. As for Dad, he maintained a safe distance from both Mom and me. He watched the news at volume 2 last night. I think it was the silence right before the storm that was to come today.

As I and my two doom-mates, Mikka and Tara, stood outside the office sweating and waiting for hell to break, our parents finally stepped out after an hour-long *meeting*. And you know how it happens that you look at your parents' facial expressions and try deciding whether to swell your chest up, or close your eyes and bury your head in the ground. Well, this was just not the moment that even a psychologist could have judged.

The five adults slowly approached us. I put on my imaginary detective lens and inspected Mom.

Her cheeks were red, but her lips weren't pursed. Confusing. Cheeks could be red both in anger and in happiness. No puckering face though.

Dad had his arm on Mom's shoulder – bold of him given the hour and place. Mixed signs!

I looked at Mikka's parents. Both seemed to have their arms held midway in the air, as if they were about to break into *Bhangra*. Confusing all the more.

I turned to look at Tara's dad. Forget it! He somehow always seemed content with Tara's performance.

Suddenly Mom leapt towards me, and I let out a shriek. She hugged me tight and exclaimed, "Bankoo ..." "... I'm so happy for you. You've been selected to continue your studies in a regular school now." Mom beamed.

I gasped and looked at Mikka and Tara. They also had got the news from their parents, and they too were shocked. Mikka could have turned into Sunny Deol from the scene *'Tareekh pe tareekh'* (haven't personally seen the movie but his cousins often tagged him in this scene's memes on Facebook). Tara handled it better... for now at least. I briefly wondered who would be crushed under her temper tantrums today.

And so here we were - Mikka, Tara and I, devastated. And as for our parents, they wore smiles wider than the girl in a toothpaste ad, finding ultimate joy in our sadness. I was certain there had been some conspiracy planned inside the office by our very own parents against their only children. But then principal ma'am, Mrs. Srivastava, came out and explained that the Special School was only for our other mates like Atul, who followed a repetitive behaviour and wanted the world to remain the same forever without an inch of change, or Chaya, who couldn't even see an elephant standing right next to her. Principal ma'am confirmed that we could now join a regular school from sixth standard onward.

But now I doubted our Principal too. I know she is a wonderful person, but I guess it was her master plan to chuck us out. Maybe she wanted to save the school from further doom. Thanks to Mikka and Tara! And, oh yes, my stars as well. Mikka's stories of all the failed unintended attempts to blow up the school, or move it altogether to a new place were never-ending. And Tara's stalkerish behaviour and temper tantrums always got the three of us in unasked-for trouble. As for me, I'd always find myself at all the wrong places at the *right* time.

As these thoughts clouded my mind during the assembly next morning, Principal ma'am took up the mike and immediately everybody in the standing queues – some on two legs, some on three or four, and those sitting on wheelchairs – fell silent.

"Good morning, everyone. As it happens every year, some of you move to regular schools for further studies. And that time of the year has come again when you will be bidding farewell to some of your good friends and mates. I have complete faith in all these children, bright in some way or the other, that they will bring a substantial change in the world and make it a better place for all of us. Wishing these 'special twenty' all the very best. Rise and shine my dears. And always remember, the limitation you put on your mind is the biggest disability of all."

The sound of claps followed.

"Twenty? So we are twenty in number?" I turned to Mikka.

"Plenty what?" Mikka asked.

I adjusted his hearing aid a bit and repeated.

"Well, got to be... if Principal ma'am said so. I still have no idea how am I on the list." Mikka looked puzzled.

Post the assembly, I wheeled to the notice board and checked the list of those *special twenty*. Rajat... Neha... Aanchal... Sahil... wait, what? They were all... good students. And then the list had our names. Was that a typo?

"Dad said we are doing well." Tara interrupted. She had joined us by the time.

"Err... and how? My last ten report cards scream average marks that I have been scoring. Mikka has almost broken, and okay fine, mended as well, all the school stuff. And you pass only when you feel like passing."

"Exactly the point!" Tara commented.

I sometimes don't understand how adults operate. The other day Mom had scolded me for scoring 63 out of 100 in Mathematics, and yesterday, after the big discussion with Principal ma'am, she was flaunting this very score with great pride to Mikka and Tara's parents.

Whatever it was, we had to accept our fate now.

But this is how it all began.

The series of unfortunate events.

A BRIEF HISTORY OF MIKKA'S TIME

Only a few people knew Mikka's real name, Mikki Singh.

In fact, only the class teacher did. After all, she couldn't ignore the attendance register. But she comfortably called him 'Mikka'. His parents, grandparents, cousins, uncles, and aunts would call him by same yet different names. That's the skill all Punjabis have, they can shuffle and alter vowels in a name and create multiple affectionate nicknames. Like Mikka has been Mikku, Mikke, Mukku and what not. In case you are trying to fit in Mukka, I won't stop you. But it's more like 'Mikka ka Mukka'. Why so? He turns green faster than the Hulk.

More facts about him:
- A car freak
- A collector of CDs (no he doesn't listen to music)
- Either found watching 'How to make...' DIYs, or HomeShop18 (what's the relation? You'll get to know soon)
- A big fan of Sunny Deol
- Mutation: Selective listening. Can choose to hear what he wants to

My first visit to Mikka's house was when I had taken a leave from school due to fever and had to jot down classwork. (Mikka is the most regular student, but when he takes leaves, we know it's *that* time of the year. Auto Expo! Yes, he will miss everything for the biggest motor show.)

I was obviously greeted with lots of love and *paranthas* by Mikka's large family, especially his dad, Jaggi uncle, *who* always seem to be in a joking mood. Jaggi uncle is the best mechanic in this part of the town and owns an Automobile repair shop and garage.

The moment I stepped into Mikka's room, I noticed three things. First, Mikka's room was more of a junkyard. Second, his walls were postered with Fast & Furious series. And third, he was watching 'Power Wheels Harley Davidson Ride on Kids Motorcycle – Unboxing and Riding'. And I knew it at that very moment, Mikka had a thing for speed.

I wheeled right next to him and waited for the fourteen-minute video to get over. During the whole time, Mikka kept uttering 'Ooo... *bhaisahab*' in different tones of excitement. And since I had no interest in watching the Harley Davidson's superfast wheels and get rubbed in, because the only parents I have didn't buy me an automated wheelchair on

my last birthday, I rather chose to stare the junk in the room. Bolts here and there, screwdrivers, plastic crap, used and broken parts of a car, an over-read pile of Fast Car magazines, CDs scattered everywhere. It was quite clear that probably Mikka aspired to join his father in the auto business... only a bit faster.

The confusion arose when Mikka switched on TV to watch HomeShop18 after the video got over. So I had to ask him. And I swear by Jarvis, this is what he told me, 'It gives me ideas. That's the only place I can see new appliances and small smart machinery. Otherwise, I have to spend time watching technicians in Papaji's garage.' Maybe Principal ma'am referred to such 'super capabilities'... quite far from my capabilities and understanding.

The real thing happened when one-day Principal ma'am and the entire class got the taste of Mikka's super abilities. Mikka was generally a happy-go-lucky guy, thanks to his genes, unless someone irritated the Hulk out of him, again, thanks to his genes. It was Khali (actually Ali Khan), the rowdy huge boy of our class, who brought out the green out of Mikka, the Hulk of St. Xavier's. Mikka, due to hearing issues, had his seat fixed in the second row (just so you know, Mikka and I can never belong to the First Benchers Association. Not our type.) And the *Khatarnaak* Khali always had his wicked eye on him. Can't actually blame Khali, Mikka attracts that kind of attention from almost everyone. The only difference is that people don't fly paper airplanes on his head, like Khali did - in every damn class. Except in the Math class, which was taken by Reddy ma'am, and Khali was never ready for Math class. Khali always entered exact ten minutes late to avoid the surprise problem-solving ritual. And I guess Mikka noticed this weakness of Khali. It was one of the rare days when it was announced that Reddy ma'am would not be taking the class on following day. Khali was absent that day, so he had no idea of the good news, and he was unpopular enough to know this from any of the classmates.

That evening I kept my colouring comic book in my bag to spend the free period next day. But Mikka sure had kept something else, something very dangerous in his bag for The Big Revenge. A Paper Airplane Launcher. Yes, a launcher made of CDs fixed onto hand fans, something and something, to get the paper planes ripping onto everything that came in their way. Next day, in the free period, the deadly weapon was placed very smartly on teacher's table while Mikka waited for *Khatam* Khali to enter. He timed it precisely. Khali was to enter in a minute and the substitute teacher, who was supposed to come from the junior wing, was to enter in five minutes. That was enough time to pull it off. As the countdown began, the entire class waited for the door to open and Khali to enter. Mikka had been making paper planes under his desk since zero period and now was ready with what seemed like a hundred paper planes. The door finally opened, and everybody waited for Khali to enter... only that he didn't, instead, Principal ma'am entered. But it was too late, Mikka had already placed the planes on the launcher by the time.

Whip... whip... whip... sweep... sweep!

Mikka's Air Force planes launched at a supersonic speed right at St. Xavier's school's Principal. They went like sharp bullets.

The whole class gasped! Including Khali who was about to enter right behind Principal ma'am but had ducked on time. Rest is history.

The chilling story is still narrated by fellow classmates to the neighbouring sections. As for Khali, he never underestimated the power of

Mikka from then on and kept his distance from him. But who knew this was just the beginning. Mikka has broken and mended a lot of school stuff since. No proofs found (thanks to Terrific Tara!), but people just knew that if something had moved at a trembling speed, or had wheels, Mikka Mechanic was behind it.

THE CURIOUS CASE OF TANTRUM TARA

While the majority of us were trying to cope up with two parents in the house, Tara Vasandani just had to deal with one. Tara's father, Sanjay Vasandani, had been by himself since times unknown. And anyway, we all thought Vasandani uncle was the coolest dad on this planet. I mean, if Tara would have asked for a weekend getaway to Moon, he would have merrily arranged that too, maybe with a slight detour to Pole Star. Instant respect for her dad when you'll know that Tara owns a Segway of her own! Yes. Hello, this side from Bankoo Bakshi, the little guy on an ordinary manual wheelchair whose parents don't even feel the need to buy their only child an automated wheelchair as they think it to be an appropriate gift for his Sixteenth Birthday, by when Tara would probably be owning a private jet of her own.

Till the time Mikka and I weren't friends with Tara, we (and the whole class) were quite traumatised by her behaviour and actions. A new teacher from Nursery wing once happened to pass by our class and caught Arpit jumping on desks. She scolded him and asked Arpit to exchange seats with Tara, who was sitting in the first row. Note that when Tara felt like sitting in the first row, the entire Front Bench Association would move back to the third row to maintain enough distance from her. Anyway, the teacher politely asked Tara to move back and make a place for Annoying Arpit. Tara didn't move. Ma'am requested her again. Tara ignored. Ma'am tapped her shoulder. Tara looked up. We all felt the tremors. Hell broke, and she shouted... at Arpit.

'Don't you understand Arpit... stop jumping like a monkey, and sit still wherever you're sitting.'

Poor Nursery ma'am turned into stone and so did Arpit. He didn't move an inch from his

seat the entire day. He only went to the loo

after school was over, that too under the supervision of his granddad who had come to pick him up. As for the poor new teacher, she was called for a quick meeting by the Principal ma'am, and so was every other new teacher. Only God knows what they discussed in that meeting. Would they chuck out Tara from school? Would she be to attend social behaviour classes in the special wing? Well, no one really knows what happened but nothing changed at all. Except for Tara, that was her last obvious tantrum. Though she got a new nickname - 'Tantrum Tara'.

If Tara didn't want to attend a class, well, she wouldn't. And no one dared say anything to her. Once, Rahul was peeping into Himani's register to cheat in Math class, when Reddy ma'am caught him. He was punished to stand for the entire period. While Tara sat right in front of ma'am, completely lost in drawing a fine switchboard on the wall of a room in a flat of a 3D building. And Reddy ma'am said nothing to her. Nothing! If this was not enough to make poor Rahul and a few others feel bad, that drawing was also displayed in the annual school exhibition and was appreciated for the eye for detail Tara had. She would score marks if she wanted to and if she didn't want to, well, that was also fine. The weird part was no teacher argued or scolded her ever, no matter what she did.

Then one day, Snooper Sneha started a rumour that Tara had put on airs about the fact that she was the only heir of Vasandani Industries and the teachers didn't say anything to her because her super-rich dad would gift all the teachers a big flat soon. When Tara got to know about this rumour, she confronted Sneha in front of the whole class. I was not there to witness the scene but Mikka was, and he called me in the evening to suggest that Tara is really good at heart and we should befriend her. The class still thought twice before talking to Tara, but Mikka and I shared the bench with her from the very next day, and now our friendship is unshakable. As for Sneha, well, her life transformed that day, and her snooping days were over.

But there is something more important that you should know. Her *mutation*. (I don't know about other classes, but this term was

quite popular among us classmates who count each other's oddities as *mutation* and tried to find something cool in it). So our friend, Terrific Tara is a Super-Spy. She can stalk anyone to death and that person won't even realise it.

The other day when her dad got free from work early, he himself came to pick her up from school in a ... (Ahem!) BMW. Mikka couldn't leave the car's side and kept staring at it as puppy love bloomed in his eyes.

"Dad, did Raju *bhaiya* enter my room last evening when I was off on my Segway?"*(No one was allowed to enter her room)*

"No kid, he was off to the market," the coolest uncle responded.

"Did you enter then?" retorted Tara.

"No, I didn't," said uncle and winked at Mikka.

"Dad, stop lying. I know either of you have entered my room. Make sure this doesn't happen again. My rules don't change on a Sunday." Tara told her dad sternly.

The next day we curiously asked Tara how she had got to know that someone had entered her room. And I swear by S.H.I.E.L.D., that's what she answered.

'I had hooked up a paper strip between the door and the wall so that if someone opens the door, the strip falls and I get to know someone has barged in.'

Mikka and my jaws dropped, and we gave up on asking any further questions.

We often wondered what the big deal about her room was. But then we concluded that since she was a girl, she had to make a great deal about anything and more so about her room. Not that we didn't make a big deal when we wanted a room of our own. Just that our rule book (which we didn't even have) never mentioned anyone taking permission from us before entering our room. Actually, it was the other way round. We had to seek permission to go to *our* room and even had to explain why we needed to shut the door.

Some days we would find Tara completely lost in her own calculations and we would be able to get nothing out of her on asking what she was up to. We asked her if this was about her room. She would just wickedly nod and get back to her murmurings and start penning down something.

This would get us all the more curious. What was she hiding? Was she building a Tara Vasandani Empire underground? Was she designing a switch-board that would give an electric shock to anyone who entered her room? Was she raising some wild raccoons for her pets?

DREADFUL DAYS AHEAD

It took us a few days to make peace with our parents' hasty decision of getting us enrolled in different schools. And soon that day also came in our lives when it was time to go to the new regular school.

Today was my Day-One. Nervous-Day-One. Actually, let me be honest, it was Dreadful-Day-One!

Dad dropped me right outside Model Public School. For a moment I sneaked a look into the car's mirror to see if I was remotely close to a 'model'.

No, I ain't, shouted my head.

I entered the gates. And I swear by Captain America, everything seemed to be irregular already.

A peon was assigned to drop me to the class. He looked dead into my face, like Uncle

Fester in Addams Family. Yes, my parents love that show and still watch it on YouTube.

As he wheeled me towards my class, I realised I was being watched by other kids around. Wait, no - I was being stared at. And I can bet my life - it was NOT a friendly stare. It was a strange stare that your dog would give if he saw a meagre new creature in your house.

After the peon dropped me to my class, I got a chance to have a proper look at him. I decided to blame the peon's sunken dark eyes and hunched back for all the strange stares. There had to be hope in the world, after all. Thankfully, being the new student, I was not asked any questions by the class teacher. This gave me a little hope that I would not be ragged or stared at and be left in peace. The class teacher showed me my table and asked me to get comfortably settled. But the next moment, she asked me to introduce myself to the entire class. My heart started racing faster than a bullet train. Tell me who's good at introductions? I wonder why introductions are so necessary. Maybe they should just distribute

pamphlets with their face on it, a few lines under and that's it. That would be less embarrassing. Somehow I gathered the courage, gulped down my saliva and managed to blabber something like this.

'Hi, my name is...Bikram Bakshi. Ummm... I came here from St. Xaviers School. I...I am ten years old and I like... DEAD SILENCE'. No, I didn't say 'dead silence', and I don't like it either. But that was the sound in the room at that time. Dead silence!

The first four periods passed by smoothly, lunch bell rang and children waited to jump like they were sitting on a spring.

But then there are only a few teachers in this world who carry the guts to make some random announcement, even when the lunch bell has rung. And Mrs. Subramaniam was one of them. She was as tall as a WWE wrestler and could easily chokeslam The Great Khali. She taught every parent's dream subject, and every student's nightmare (no offence to the first benchers). MATHEMATICS!

Even when the lunch bell rang, not a single student gathered the courage to get up. They just sat still and waited.

"Boys and girls, I have an announcement to make so don't leave your seats yet."

Students sighed. Mrs. Subramaniam continued.

"We have an interclass basketball competition coming up next month. So meet your P.T. sir and form up your team. Give me the final list of names soon. Your next few P.T. periods will be spent practising for the competition."

Basketball competition was coming up!

This was my chance to shine.

Maybe I could make some friends this way. After all, I used to play fairly well at the friendly matches we used to have at Xavier's. I wondered how different could this be. (HINT: different, very different. I'll get back to it soon.)

The teacher finally left, and the class came back to life again. Suddenly I realised, the focus was back on me. Everyone stared at me and my wheelchair. I wished the teacher had introduced me saying something like, 'Boys and girls, this is Bankoo Bakshi and his wheelchair, Willy Bakshi. They will be studying in this class from now on. Please be good to both of them and DO NOT STARE.'

No one came up to me to start a conversation. So I decided to take my awkwardness and my lunchbox out of the class with me. Perhaps the aroma of the food in the corridor would act like a people-magnet, and someone might end up asking for one bite. And that one bite might turn into a conversation, and that conversation might turn into friendship. And then there won't be any Day-One Blues.

And so I opened my bag to take out the lunchbox. Couldn't find it.

Not possible, I myself had taken it from Deenu *kaka* and kept it in my bag.

It was not there. I checked all the pockets and checked my desk.

Not there.

Whaaaaaat?!!! I was robbed off my tiffin box on day one?! I was robbed off the only way of making any friends and getting myself through these uncomfortable, unpleasant, embarrassing, awkward, vexing periods.

I should have been introduced by the Principal!

Coming back to basketball. It was different, very different.

It was P.T. period after lunch, and everyone gathered excitedly at the basketball court. Mr. O.P.D. Singh gave instructions to the boys for the competition. Wait... Yes... I know... That's right... No... I'd heard it right... Trust me. His name is 'O.P.D' with a Singh. Om Prakash Daman Singh.

"Joydeep will be the captain of the team, and he will do the team selection. Please cooperate with him," announced Mr. Singh as he left for the other side of the court to give similar instructions to the girls.

Joydeep was a tall, well-built boy, who looked like the dude of the school. Or should I say the 'ideal model' of Model Public School. The amount of attention he had grabbed from both boys and girls since period one was directly proportional to the stares I had got during the entire day. He announced again that he will be the captain of the team and will choose the team. Everyone nodded... and bowed. One by one, the boys went forward to showcase their basketball skills.

Finally, it was my turn as I was next in the queue. I was more nervous than ever. Should I dribble a bit and then basket... or should I straight away take a shot? Let me just dribbb...

"You, you're blocking the way. You can move out of the court and watch from there." said the captain of the team.

"But I also want to be a part of the team."

"Ya right, why don't you try next year? I don't have time for all this." barked Cheap Joydeep.

It was humiliation straight in the face. The next in queue went forward and took the shot.

I wheeled out of the court.

TARA'S FORBIDDEN FORTRESS

If there's any connection stronger than the one between mothers and their children, it is the one between mothers and the lunch boxes.

"Next time you lose your lunch box, I will give you lunch in a *Haldiram Dabba* Bankoo!" Mom yelled at me. Tell me if it was my mistake.

"Now leave for school, you're getting late. And listen, Tara had called. It's her birthday today, and she has invited you to her birthday party in the evening. I've told Deenu *kaka* to take you to her house at 6 o'clock. Be ready by the time." Mom added.

Heck! I had forgotten again that it was Tara's birthday. She is my best friend after all. But you know how it is with boys and dates. Not my mistake again.

Deenu *kaka* wheeled me towards school which was just ten minutes from my place. I was already waiting for school to get over. I was dying to meet Tara and Mikka. I remembered how cool our life was in St. Xavier's school. It wasn't ever tough being Mikka's friend, you just had to be a great listener. Any which way, your talks would hardly reach his tough ears, so he didn't care much about what you were really saying.

I wondered what would Vasandani uncle gift Tara on her tenth birthday. Of course, he had already bought her almost anything she wanted - all the gadgets and all the remotes and what not. I recalled how on her sixth birthday, uncle had invited the entire class to a fancy restaurant on her birthday party. And this had been the trend since. Thanks to Super-Vasandani uncle, we have been to Hotel The Ashok, The Oberoi, Shangri La Hotel and The Taj. And that is how we got to know something more about Tara. She had a more serious problem than anyone of us did. I don't know how to name that problem but uncle told us something like if she started working on something she would not leave it in between at any cost, because that would irritate her and she won't be able to sleep. And that her tantrums were a part of her health problem though she didn't mean any of it. They were seeing a doctor, and she was slowly being treated, and she may not get completely fine, but she would always be a good person. I didn't doubt that. She was really nice inside, and a total crack outside.

We had almost arrived at the school gates. I wondered where the party was this year. I guess Mom had told me but I had probably missed it.

"Deenu *kaka*, which restaurant are we going to for Tara's birthday party?" I quickly asked before entering the gates of Mod-*hell* Public School.

"No restaurant. We are going to her house," answered Deenu *kaka*.

Whaaat? Her house?! This can't be happening. Tara can never invite us to her house.

Deenu *kaka* would have heard it wrong. I thought of calling Mom to confirm the venue.

"Deenu *kaka*, please call Mom, I need to talk to her."

.

.

"Mom, where did Tara say, she is hosting her birthday party?" I asked while I sheepishly avoided looking at Deenu *kaka*.

"Her house this time," Mom confirmed.

UNBELIEVABLE.

I was already sure that it would be the longest day at school today. What I didn't realise that it would be a major grey day too.

1. My tiffin box disappeared again.

2. I almost soiled my pants in the bathroom because Sarla aunty, our school *aaya*, was busy eyeing our school gardener instead of helping me. I was saved by a fraction of a second. GOD EXISTS.

3. It was drawing class and everyone (including the Art teacher) somehow had an expectation that I'll be really

good at drawing. People and their stereotypes I tell you. I think they were expecting a *Taare Zameen Par* out of me. We were asked to draw a scenery and not that I didn't draw mountains and rivers and the sun shining bright. It's just that it all looked like the inner parts of a car when you open the bonnet. GOD DOESN'T EXIST.

I had only survived today because I knew I'll be meeting Tara and Mikka in the evening.

The afternoon nap wasn't very comfortable either. The entire afternoon I helplessly dreamt of Tara's room. In one of the dreams, she wore Harry Potter glasses and hid an anaconda in her room and they both talked in hisses. In the other dream, she looked more like Mikka and was preparing to launch rocket from her room that didn't have a roof. But the weirdest of all was this. I see Tara entering her room and leave the door half shut. Out of curiosity both Mikka and I peep into the room through the slight gap and we see bright light coming out from one of the walls. As we muster the guts to enter her room, we see a small door in the wall from where the blinding light is breaking in and Tara is stepping out through that door. We hurriedly follow her. As we follow her through that door in the wall, we are suddenly at a whole new place and Tara's house has vanished. Instead, we find ourselves entering the huge gates of... 'TARALAND'. We see Tara disappearing behind a massive glass building. Our jaws drop as we start to look up at the massive shiny building. There are trains flying in the sky. Not the usual trains. These look extravagant and splendid. Bright red coloured compartments, golden window frames, clear glasses, and written in gold - Tara Express. As we adjust our eyes back onto ground level, Mikka goes bonkers. A BMW in the colour yellow and green has stopped by to ask us for a ride. A BMW for an auto rickshaw! We look at the roads in amazement. There are indeed so many auto rickshaws just that they are Mercedes and

Jaguars. People around are crossing roads on their Segway and we seem to be the only ones on foot. Suddenly everyone breaks into chorus, 'Happy Birthday to You! Happy Birthday to You!' and Tara appears out of nowhere, grabbing me and Mikka by our shoulder and asking for her birthday gift.

"Bankoooo, get up! You've overslept. Get ready for Tara's birthday party. And here's her gift, don't forget to take this along," roared Mom, literally throwing me out of the bed. And then she claims to be the calmest mom in the world.

Deenu *kaka* made me reach Tara's house quite on time. She had a huge house. I was sure she had a huge room too. Would she show me the room? Had she already shown it to Mikka? Where were they both?

The party was as usual fancy and with children I had never seen in my life. I entered the hall and saw Tara. She was giving a very bad stare to one of the kids who was constantly jumping on her bear-sized couch. Mikka intervened and pulled her out of the scene. He then pointed towards me. Tara looked at me and her expressions suddenly changed into a smile. It was such a delight to be together again.

"So how is it going you guys?" chirruped Tara.

Err... Okay. She seemed to be in a relatively good mood today. Or was she having fun in her new school? Without us?! Her father had got her admission in one of the best schools in the town. And it was just understood she won't be ragged. She had zero tolerance for things anyway.

Mikka adjusted his hearing aid and started, "you mean school right?"

"Not that great." He continued. "It is quite different from our school you know. I'll definitely take time to adjust. For the first time I'm happy I cannot hear properly. Somehow they always have something to talk or whisper... I don't know which one. Today at the assembly, one of the prefects came up to me and pounced at my hearing aid. That idiot dragged me to the teacher and complained that I was listening to music. He had it from the teacher of course and I was asked to go back. My hearing aid has not been working properly since", sighed poor Mikka.

Mikka's father had got his admission in Government Boys School. Being a local mechanic he couldn't afford Mikka's education like Tara's father or even like mine. Mikka never scored above average grades in class, but he was good at learning his dad's work. And that is all that mattered for him and his family. Mikka's dad often joked, 'oye, that's okay if you can't hear much, you'll be away from the world's nuisances.'

"Leave your hearing aid with me tonight, and pick it up tomorrow," said Tara.

"Why? What will you do?" asked Mikka curiously.

"I'll add supersonic capabilities to it. You'll be able to hear the slightest of sounds then. Just knock your *dhai-killo-ka-hath* on anyone who talks cheap about you after that", answered Tara.

"What? Have you lost it? Don't you pull my leg, I'm telling you." Mikka was already fuming up and could cross the boiling point of water anytime now.

Strangely, Tara was still calm! Such days exist.

Tara continued, "You both have never seen my room right? Come, I'll show you guys." Our jaws dropped hearing this.

She pushed us out of the Hall. Mikka and I couldn't help exchange looks. Mikka seemed as thrilled as I was. Probably he too had spent the afternoon dreaming about Tara's forbidden room and the wild creatures she might be hiding inside.

"What do you think is in there?" I asked Mikka, as Tara was busy leading us to the room.

"I don't know dude. I don't even know how to play music in case we find Fluffy, the three-headed dog in the restricted area. I wish Harry Potter was there with us," answered Mikka. For a moment I thought I should have probably bid a warmer goodbye to my parents before leaving for Tara's place.

Tara opened the door to her room. There was no blinding light bursting out of a wall.

There was no bed either.

Instead, what we saw was:

1. A big Apple desktop.
2. Another large LED screen connected through millions of wires to gadgets I don't even know the names of.
3. A few video cams here and there.
4. Weird mobiles and walkie-talkies.

Who was she – Tony Stark?!

"O beta, what is this?" blurted Mikka as he looked around jumping and sprinting.

"This is my laboratory," claimed Tara.

"Laboratory? And what do you do? Are you a detective? Do you have a chip in your body? Don't you sleep?" asked Mikka impatiently.

I had lost it too but decided to keep my mouth shut. Mikka should be enough.

"Relax Mikka. And of course, I sleep dumbo! Family doctor says I am suffering from Hyper-focus. And this is where my focus gets to be. I like doing this stuff. I can hack people's systems, I can fit GPS into things, I can invent a few small gadgets of my own, and I can control another few gadgets too. This has fascinated me since very early," explained Hi-Tech Tara.

"Woh maaaaaaan!" is all we could blurt out. I was mostly still trying to understand the sentence.

Mikka said he remembered Iron Man, Krishna from Koi Mil Gaya, Stephen Hawking and Einstein all at once. I wondered why she was an average student at school. Probably Physics hadn't started yet.

Tara told us a few stories of how she had caught Raju *bhaiya* having an affair with the neighbour's maid, Pooja *didi*. He would go missing every day from 5 PM to 6 PM to take her to the vegetable market on his bicycle which has an experimental GPS fit in it and of which Raju *bhaiya* still has no idea about. From then on he had to bring chocolates for Tara so that she keeps his secret well. The funny part is, when he goes somewhere else on a particular day, Tara tells him of the place he went to the next day, and this gets Raju *bhaiya* really scared. He keeps thinking how Tara could get to know of the place as he doesn't even carry a smartphone, but Tara only giggles away.

Mikka still refused Hi-Tech Tara's offer of supersonic hearing aid. He said hearing to so many unnecessary things will disturb his mental peace. I didn't deny that.

They both looked at me for my new school stories. I told them what all I went through. The disappearing lunch box routine, the unfriendly classmates, and most sadly, the basketball episode.

"How dare he chuck you out of the basketball court?!" Mikka had turned into Tara Singh from the movie *Gadar* now.

"*Oye* listen, you leave your wheelchair with me next weekend. Let me do something with it."

"But what's the problem with my wheelchair?"

"*Arrey*, you just wait and watch. I am not an idiot spending so much time with my dad and his workers at the garage. Tara has motivated me to follow my passion. No one can stop my friend now.

Khelega tu basketball![1] Jo bole so nihaaaal..." Mikka Mechanic stood up with his fist help up high.

You will play basketball!

MIKKA'S MARVEL

It was Sunday, and Deenu *kaka* had dropped me at Mikka's place early morning. Mikka was as excited about my wheelchair 'transformation' as I was confused.

We went to the garage right at the back of his house. He asked his dad not to send anyone to his 'private corner' of the garage. He will be working along with Bobby *bhaiya*, his dad's assistant.

What on Earth was he up to? Making a Transformer - out of my wheelchair?

Anyway, his dad said yes to all his requests. I guess he was too indulged in his butter soaked *aaloo paranthas* and the intoxicating glass of *lassi*.

We entered the garage and Mikka helped me sit on the couch while Bobby *bhaiya* observed my wheelchair. Mikka took him to a corner and started explaining him something. I could see Bobby *bhaiya's* eyes opening wider and wider with each line Mikka spoke and each hand expression he made.

WHAT WAS HE UP TO?

I hesitantly reminded Mikka to not destroy my wheelchair. So what if it was not automatic, it was my dad's gift, and I didn't want to give my parents any shock. But Mikka didn't respond to it. I realised he was not wearing his hearing aid. Damn it!

I don't even remember when I fell asleep watching these guys loosening or tightening up the bolts of my wheelchair.

Sun was at its peak when I got up with the smell of hot *paranthas*. Lunch had come for both of us. Mikka joined on the couch with me. There's something about the Punjabi *paranthas* and white butter. They're irresistible! And you're bound to sleep after such heavy treat.

I didn't even dare take a glance at my wheelchair before dozing off for another long afternoon nap.

It was 6 PM, and the roads had come to life with all the honking and vrooming. Deenu *kaka* was to come in an hour to take me back home.

I looked around for my wheelchair. It stood there in the corner. Mikka and Bobby *bhaiya* were enjoying tea break. They had this smile on their faces which I really couldn't understand. But it looked like an accomplished one. I looked at my wheelchair again, this time with more focus. Somehow it didn't look like it had been changed even one bit.

I looked again.

No change.

NO CHANGE!

What had they done? Opened it up for their own fun bit and put it back together again?

For a moment that sulking feeling creeped in. I had been mocked by my own friend. A friend with a similar physical situation, probably less daunting, had pulled a cheap joke on me. Perhaps he just wanted to explore another sort of 'wheel' for his own recreation. I was such an idiot to have fallen in such a trap.

I felt like crying. Why did I have high hopes for even a second? It was all my mistake. All my life I had got those sympathetic stares from everyone. For once, just once, I hoped to feel like an ordinary kid for whom things were possible, and life was faster.

Mikka noticed that I was up. He left his teacup and came up to me, with a wide smile on his face.

"Are you ready Bankoo?" he still had that accomplished smile. I was furious but confused.

"What do you mean?" I asked, tears still in my throat.

"For your TURBO!" said Mikka.

"Turbo?! What's that?" I couldn't understand.

"Tch! Your wheelchair *yaar*." Mikka pointed out towards my wheelchair.

"My wheelchair?! But it looks just the same." I still managed to speak.

"Can you speak a bit louder? My hearing aid is still giving me problems and I cannot lip read such a long sentence." Mikka said while fidgeting with his hearing aid.

"It-looks-just-the-same." I repeated with pauses.

"That's the thing, my friend. Never underestimate a wheelchair by only its wheels and a seat." Mikka was as excited as Sunny Deol in that song 'yaara o yaara... *milna hamara*'.

Mikka waved at Bobby *bhaiya* who quickly brought the wheelchair to me and helped me sit on it. Mikka pushed a green button on my wheelchair. That button wasn't there before.

My wheelchair kicked off like a motorbike.

Dhroom... Dharoom... Dhrrooom...

I was shocked. My jaws dropped. Could this even happen?

"Oye Bankoo, now listen", said Mikka in a serious tone.

"I have fit motor into your wheelchair. This green button will switch the motor on. The gears on the left can be increased from one to five. This is to increase the speed up to five levels. The other lever on the right is to rotate your wheelchair, if you push it back, then it will move backwards."

I was speechless. Was I dreaming?

After thirty seconds of staring at the lever, a red button caught my eye. I stretched my finger to press it.

"Don't," commanded Mikka, my coolest mechanic ever. "It's the last resort. Moreover, we don't have enough space here in the garage. Let's go out."

"What is it for?" I asked.

"It pulls the Super Boosters on!" said Mikka.

"Whaaaaat? You have fit super boosters in my wheelchair? Was the motor speed not enough?" I was more than content with the automatic functioning wheelchair. But super boosters... they sounded out of this world.

Mikka's eyes were shining. "I had to try it *yaar*. I'm trying to fit one on my skates as well. It would be so cool to see you wheeling at super speed... Like wooooooooooshhhh!!!" I guess Mikka wanted me to be some Flying *Jatt* or something. I haven't even seen the movie.

Mikka asked me to pull gear one and guided me out of the garage. It was dark by now and there weren't many people around. He made me try gears two to five, rotate and back gear. I was on could number nine. I felt like the coolest guy on Earth. Everything felt so possible, so achievable. I didn't have words to thank Mikka. He was a great friend and a brilliant-mechanic-in-the-making.

An empty ground had come by the time I got over trying gear five. Mikka came running.

"It's time to press the red button. Before you push start, let me tell you how to stop it. You'll press the red button again, and the Super Booster will automatically switch off. You will return to normal speed then," instructed Mikka. He took two steps backward and wished me luck.

My heart was beating faster than ever. I rotated my chair towards an emptier space and pressed the red button.

Swoooooooshhhhh... Zaaappp!!!!

Was it the speed of a bullet?! Alright, I'm exaggerating.

But it was super-duper fast. I could have competed with a scooty I guess.

I pushed the red button off right before I was about to hit the fence, and wheeled back to Mikka at gear five.

He was doing Bhangra!!

I was dancing too. My one hand in the air and the other on the gear, moving forward and backward and rotating from left to right. Does that count as dancing? IT SURE AS HELL DOES!

After we were done celebrating like crazies, we made a pact of not telling about this to anyone, except to Tara of course. Our newly launched rule book said:

1. No flaunting in the school (that meant I had to sacrifice being a part of the basketball team)

2. No stunts in front of parents (because their life is chaotic, they are too calculative, and they are just a bunch of negative people around us kids)

3. The newly acquired *superpower* will only be used for greater good (because I'm the good guy)

4. We are of the society and for the society (I will save the world from bad, Mikka is my Robin and I'm Batman!)

Soon Deenu *kaka* arrived to take me back home. At the dinner table with Mom-Dad, I told them how good the *paranthas* at Mikka's place tasted, and that I could have them all day long. (And sleep all day long under the influence of heavily intoxicated and yummiest ever glass of *lassi*.) Mom promised me that she will prepare some *paneer paranthas* for my lunchbox tomorrow. It just struck me if I would have told that Mikka's mom served me the cheesiest ever pizza, would she have prepared the same for my lunchbox. I don't know, worth a try for next time maybe. But then why would a Punjabi make pizzas when they have butter dipped *paranthas* under their belt?

Anyway, Dad finally helped me into my room and bid me goodnight.

It was a long day, and it finally sinked in. My dream had come true.

I was sitting on an automated wheelchair!

MY automated wheelchair.

MY TURBO!

TWEAKING TURBO

I had to show TURBO to Tara.

I told mom I wanted to go to Tara's house after school. She promised she would let me go but only if I went to buy vegetables all by myself from the local market quite near to our house. I thumbed up. Mom had started giving me these small tasks every few days so that I could build up my confidence and be more independent.

I didn't mind at all now. I had Turbo with me.

School was the usual. And the P.T. period too. I could have flaunted my wheelchair to Cheap Joydeep and his basketball team and most probably bagged a place in the team too with my new speed skills, but somehow it didn't feel the right thing to do. The rule book said no flaunting. Unless there would come a day when O.P.D. Sir would kick Cheap Joydeep so far out of the basketball team that the world would need me to fetch him back from the end of the road to hell before he gets rolled right into a blazing fire. Because I'm the good guy. I am the Turbo Guy. And the Turbo Guy is the bigger person who saves everyone.

Except at lunchtime.

Yes, you guessed it right. I couldn't save my lunchbox, and it got stolen again. The precious *paranthas* had vanished, the box was nowhere to be seen. Why god why? Why with me? Don't I deserve a good mid-meal?

I knew I would be bringing out a demon out of my mother today when she would get to know that I was robbed again. The thought got me sweating already.

Only one thing could save me now. My pocket money.

Maybe I could ask Deenu *kaka* to take me to a nearby market, and I could buy another lunchbox. But I needed to buy a ditto copy of the lunchbox so that Mom didn't get one bit suspicious. And the probability of that was pretty less. I mean who would keep a Kung-Fu

Panda lunchbox when the Minions had taken over the plastic world.

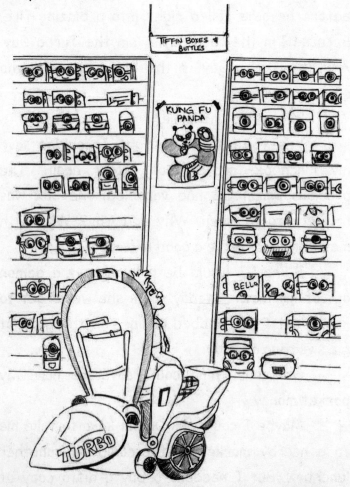

And so money couldn't buy everything.

I made peace with reality and left directly for home with Deenu *kaka*. I thought of dashing into my room on fourth gear since Mom Dad were in office and the house was all mine, but then the voice of the microwave oven got me back into reality as Deenu *kaka* heated up my lunch that Mom had cooked before leaving for office. Maybe I should think of discussing a certain 'Me-Time' zone with Deenu *kaka* but the last month I discussed the same with Mom, it didn't go really well. After my Mom's strict 'No, you don't need it.' I was kept a close eye upon. If I took more than five minutes in loo, Deenu *kaka* would be asked to knock on the loo door and check upon me. If I went to bed before the usual time, to just play the next level of my video game so I could have a good night's sleep, I would find my dad's head peeping into the room to closely understand my definition of 'Me-Time'. I think the one thing parents all over the world are most scared about and can't even avoid its incoming is the Teenage. The weird part was I am not even a Tween yet. So I concluded that it was useless discussing the point.

Anyway, evening came and it was time for us to leave for Tara's place now. I felt like telling Deenu *kaka* that I can go by myself, now that Turbo was with me, but that would have made him sad. So I let him wheel me down to her place.

Tara was glad to see me. I somehow expected her to be behaving like a maniac after seeing me, but then I realised she had no idea about my *new* life and my *automated* wheelchair. I guess even Mikka hadn't got the chance to tell Tara of our action-packed weekend.

"Tara, I have to show you something. Take me to your laboratory," I told her. Of course, I could go in a flash by myself but I chose to keep the secret a bit longer.

Deenu *kaka* and Raju *bhaiya* got busy in their conversations as Tara wheeled me into her roomatory.

"Here you are. Now tell me, what is it?" demanded Tara wide-eyed. Probably she was expecting that I would tell her I've finally found my lunchboxes, or that I have been asked by the school Principal to be the new captain of the basketball team, or that I have put my parents up for adoption.

"What is it Bankoo? Tell me before I lose my patience," pressed Tara.

Oh. I forgot that making Tara wait could turn things ugly.

I didn't want to trigger her tantrum button on. So I pressed the green button of my wheelchair on. Motor roared. (Okay not actually roared, but came to life... and that was kind of enough for me). I pulled the lever to two. (Tara had a huge room... I mean, laboratory... so the stunts were doable). Then I pressed the lever of the wheelchair to move backward and then I rotated it.

Tara went bonkers and jumped up and down on the bed of wires scattered on the floor.

"Are you kidding me? How did you get that? It's the same chair, isn't it? Did you get it remade by someone?"

"Yes Tara, and that someone is Mikka, the coolest mechanic ever. He transformed my wheelchair into TURBO. Remember Mikka had asked me to get my wheelchair to his garage last weekend?" And I told Tara all the details of the day, including the yummy *paranthas* and *lassi*.

"What are you saying? This is unbelievable," said Tara.

"I know. I have gone bonkers too! But wait till you see this." As I said this, I pressed the red button on. (Don't worry, I had enough practice stopping Turbo at the right time to keep myself from banging into a wall or something.)

Wooooooshh.... Zaaappp!!! Screeeechhh!

I managed to stop right in front of her Apple desktop.

"SUPER BOOSTERS!! Mikka fit THAT in your chair?! Oh boy, whosoever thought he was useless... needs to see this!" Tara had already fallen off her bean bag.

She tried the wheelchair herself. And as she did, she started jotting down something on a piece of paper. I was sitting merrily on the bean bag with a cup of hot chocolate in my hand and didn't feel like asking her what she was up to.

She leapt across the roomatory to get all sorts of things from boxes and almirahs and then gazed at my wheelchair ambitiously. Oh god, what exactly was this girl up to?

"Umm... Tara, what's on your mind?" I asked Tara, not trying to offend her. It could get risky you know.

Tara didn't answer. I thought of postponing the idea of asking again.... until she brought a LIQUID FIXER.

I had to ask her now!

"Tara, what are you up to?"

Tara walked up to me with her famous How-Dare-You-Question-Me expression and started off.

"Dude, what do you think? With those crazy super boosters on, would you not need a seat belt? In case you lose control or something gets dysfunctional, should your Turbo not have a GPS system to track you down? What about your safety now that you could be all alone? What if your wheelchair breaks down in the middle of the road and you get stuck? Don't you think you should have a pocket to keep your crutches as well, just in case?"

Each of her questions made sense. If only she could work on her facial expressions.

She continued, "I have fit a GPS tracking system under your seat. I am fitting a seat belt to your chair, and an elastic pocket on the back, where you can keep your crutches. I am also fitting two cans under the armrest which will spring out at face level on tapping hard. One of them will shoot out sharp nails..."

"Wooh! And what about the other one?"

"It's a pepper spray."

"Oh no Tara, not that pink bottle of yours. It's so girlie! I cannot have anything pink on Turbo."

Why is pink even a colour? Who was crazy enough to mix white in red? I whined in my head.

"Shut up Bankoo, don't argue with me. It's for your own safety. Remember how we are taught about safety from strangers and taking care of ourselves," preached Tara.

It was useless arguing with her. So I let her do whatever she wanted to. I decided to detach that pink pepper spray and throw it in a sewer on my way back home.

Deenu *kaka* knocked the roomatory's door. It was time to go home. Tara had made whatever additions to the wheelchair by the time, and Turbo looked ready. I bid Tara a quick goodbye, happy that Turbo and I were finally rid of her and soon Turbo would be rid of that stupid pink pepper spray bottle as well.

As Deenu *kaka* got me wheeling back home, I started looking for a sewer or a garbage bin. Finally spotting a town dumpyard just across the road, I requested Deenu *kaka* to wheel me near to it so that I could throw my chewing gum (and the ridiculous pepper spray bottle) there and not mess the road. *Kaka* did so and started wheeling me towards the dumpyard when his mobile rang.

"Hello *bitiya*, yes one minute," answered Deenu *kaka* and handed over the phone to me.

"Don't even think of going to the dumpyard and throwing off my pretty pink pepper spray. Don't forget I have a GPS on your chair to track you now," threatened the voice from the other end.

It was Terror Tara.

"Yeah, of course. I am heading towards home only. Don't worry, I'll be safe." I replied.

"Great. Bubye!"

I suggested Deenu *kaka* a better idea of straight away heading for home since we were already late. He didn't mind.

The weather at home didn't look very pleasant. I realised I was surrounded by black thunder clouds and Mom was about to burst on me. Guess the reasons:

Reason One - I had lost my tiffin box again, and I was a careless, useless fellow. There is no justice in this world.

Reason Two – I had spent too much time at Tara's house and had forgotten to buy vegetables.

Will women ever understand men?

THE MiDNiGHT RENDEZVOUS

Model Public School didn't get any unnecessary attention from me now. We shared a very formal relationship. I went to School, teachers gave me homework, students gave me stares and that's it. No school friends, no expectations, low maintenance life. But I did have a night life! Yes. I was a student by the day, a homework doer by the evening, and a stuntman by the night.

Where? The garage. My garage. Actually Dad's. But he never used it. And I was his heir, so lawfully it would belong to me. I could ask Dad to hand me over the keys, but I knew he wouldn't, since he kept gardening tools in the trunk and they could accidentally fall on me, or I could fall on them. And I would have asked for the garage to be added in his Will but that would be too rude of me to ask. So I assumed it to be mine already and swept off the keys from his long forgotten key box.

When everyone slept off at around 11 PM, I would sneak out into the garage at precisely 11:59 PM to practise. Because practice makes a man perfect, and I wanted to be perfect with Turbo. I wanted it to be a part of me. And so 12 AM to 1 AM was my Me-Time which no one knew about. That is until I told Mikka and Tara about it.

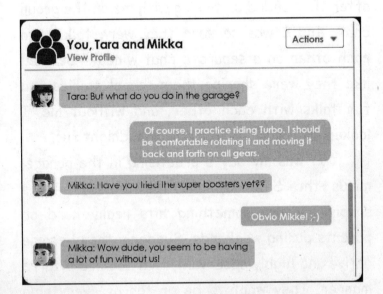

You, Tara and Mikka
View Profile

Actions ▼

Tara: But what do you do in the garage?

Of course, I practice riding Turbo. I should be comfortable rotating it and moving it back and forth on all gears.

Mikka: Have you tried the super boosters yet??

Obvio Mikke! ;-)

Mikka: Wow dude, you seem to be having a lot of fun without us!

(There was silence on the Facebook chat window for a short while. Then a sudden ping from Tara popped up.)

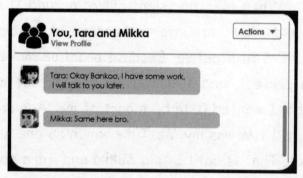

For all I know, they were both online long after they ended up talking with me on the group chat. And I was so sure they were talking to each other on a separate chat window. Seemed like they were sharing their school stories and fun talks with each other, and without me. I looked at Turbo and waited for midnight fun.

It was my day 5 practising in the garage, minus the Saturday and the Sunday. That's simply because something hits really hard on parents during weekends. Suddenly they become active and highly observant, that too in a bizarre manner. They want to be on top of everything and yet keep on pointing that this is their time to relax, and focus on other things beyond work. Which precisely means focussing on me and relaxing with me. So a couple of funny, non-ten-year-old-friendly games get lined up, and if I don't show interest, then I'm tagged lazy, and Mom concludes that probably that is why my lunchbox gets stolen. Movies with moral messages are forced upon and if I yawn watching them, or instead demand for an English movie, like maybe a Spider-Man, or The Dark Knight, my parents end up exchanging looks. They even hold a quick discussion session somewhere in the corner of the Hall to give their own U/A vs. A rating to the demanded movie. And if I am granted the permission to watch that movie, and there comes a scene during which I'm abruptly asked to fetch water for Mom who's already sipping onto some hot cup of coffee... well, then I know that scene playing in the movie has been rated A certificate by my parents, the super-secret board members of Central Board of Film Certification.

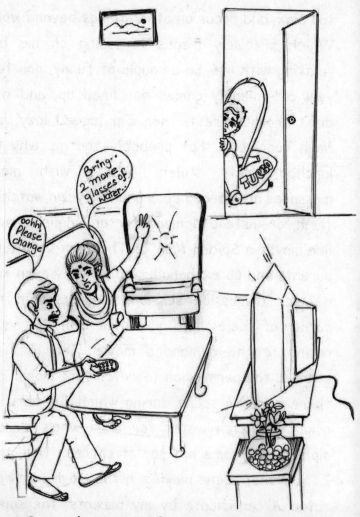

So to keep it safe and not sorry, they bribe me into watching The Jungle Book instead. But tell me if it is justifiable to watch a kid jumping onto trees and crossing bridges in a mere red cloth for a pair of briefs? It sometimes gets me wondering, who taught him to cover just that part of the body when he was raised amongst wolves and hadn't seen any human until much later. But when you can't find an answer, just call it Fiction. And that's what Fiction is all about. Like I fictionate on those missing scenes while I'm fetching Mom some water.

Anyway, the clock hit 11:59 PM and it was my time to ride Turbo out of the house into the garage without making even the slightest sound. Of course, I was thankful to the AC in my parents' room to be highly cooperative by being louder than my wheels. Mom had asked me to practise gratitude at all times and this was definitely the time.

I entered the garage and latched the door from inside. It obviously needed courage for what I had been doing since the past 4 days, but you got to do what you got to do when you know you might need to save the world someday. Or so I hoped. And for that, I had to practise.

Wham!

The noise came from outside the door followed by a knock.

A KNOCK!

Who would have knocked? Mom-Dad? I gulped. My superhero career was over in an instant. I couldn't save the world anymore. I would die an ordinary death. Tonight.

There was a stronger knock on the door this time, and I could only get a few seconds to plan the lamest ever excuse to my parents. 'Mom, Dad. I thought it would be a good idea to actually grow vegetables in the garden. The other day I couldn't help Mom by going and buying vegetables. So I thought of surprising you both with growing some.'

"Open the door Bankoo!" The female voice was definitely familiar but not that of Mom's.

"It's us – Mikka and Tara," shouted Mikka from outside.

I breathed a sigh of relief and opened the door. The brain was still in shock though.

"What are you both doing here?" I shouted as I opened the door.

"Same as what you are doing. Sneaking out," said Mikka.

"You can't practise without us. Every superhero needs a tracker and an inventor," said Tara dramatically, as she parked her Segway into the garage.

We all looked at each other for a moment, not believing that we had actually sneaked out from our houses. It was a daring act. We all let out a nervous laughter.

Mikka told us how he put the volume a bit high of his HomeShop18 TV channel and jumped out of his ground floor window. There are so many relatives living in his house that anyone in the joint family would hardly even care to notice. He got here on his pair of skates, the ones on which he was trying to fit a pair of mini super boosters. I wondered what it would actually be like after he would be able to actually fix them together. And as for Tara, well, her dad never entered her room between 10 PM and 6 AM.

"So is that a deal guys?" asked Tara.

"What deal?" I asked.

"This will be our secret meeting place," confirmed Tara

"But I am already good at practising now. I can perfectly drive Turbo and can handle stuff by myself."

"So then we will give you the stuff to handle."

"What stuff?"

Tara held out a piece of paper from her pocket and handed it over to me. This is how it read:

Case 1: That of the lecher at the college bus stop

Case 2: That of the missing dog of Mrs. Mistry

Case 3: That of the horrible Vasooli Boss

"What cases are these?" I asked curiously.

"The cases to be solved by us," answered Tara.

"In the words of Spider-Man; with great power comes great responsibility. So we have decided to use our wheel-power to put to greater good. We will do whatever we can to save our neighbourhood from evil," added Mikka, his eyes shining bright.

This sounded like a perfect plan. Dad used to tell me when he was a kid he used to play Detective with his neighbourhood friends and they would try solving some funny Contessa Car Case for months. Contessa was an old car parked right behind his ancestral house since ages, and no one knew who the owner was. He and his friends would run around the car trying to find clues of whose dumped car it was. As he would tell me his funny adventurous stories, I would imagine myself right there playing with him. Just that I couldn't imagine myself running around. And that would kill my imagination.

But guess what? Not anymore. Forget running, I could wheel.

We had real cases to solve now. We were going to do some really important work, we were going to save the society. And we held a big secret. We, the new superheroes. Tara, the Tracker. Mikka, the Inventor. And I, the Rider.

"It's a deal!" I said.

CAESAR AND THE CREEP AT THE BUS STOP

Mikka and I both have sisters. He has a sister in every colony of Jalandhar, and I, well, I too have my cousins in Chandigarh. The last time I met them was when I was about four and our parents took us all to the Rock garden. So all I am trying to say is, we know how it feels when someone bad eyes your sister.

I gave this exact reason to Tara, who wanted us to feel the emotions for the victim so that it helped us solve the case whole-heartedly. But she shook her head and said that I was talking all crap. She said that I won't even be remembering my cousin sisters' faces. Which, by the way, was true, but that doesn't stop them from being my sisters, I tried explaining.

Mikka stayed in a joint family and was quite used to having big sisters so he would better understand the feeling, she concluded.

Tara wanted to give this case to Mikka because of the Sunny Deol effects he would put to the situation and probably drive away that irritating lecher. She wanted me to concentrate more on finding Mrs. Mistry's dog, Caesar, or Scissor. I don't know which one. Yes, imagine! So, I thought of voicing it out.

"No dude." I announced in our next midnight meeting at my garage.

"What - No?"

"I cannot take the case of the lost dog of Mrs. Mistry?"

"Why can't you?"

"Because... Because... I am scared of dogs."

"Who's scared of a Labrador, for god's sake?"

"I am."

"Bankoo, you are not! You have your childhood pictures of playing in the park with this very dog from about 5 years ago. Mrs.

Mistry still remembers pushing your wheelchair behind Caesar while you guys played chase."

"She does?" This got me emotional.

"Yes. She was showing me photos the other day as she asked me about your well-being. You were about five I guess."

"But I've grown up now."

"No. You better grow up now. No case is big or small. I will add this clause in our rule book." Tara scribbled hastily in a red diary and threw back the 'rule book' on me.

Wow. So she had already *made* the Rule Book. When did she get all that time?

Anyway, it was again no point arguing with Tormenting Tara. I told her that I'll give it a thought. She got up and left at that very moment on her Segway. Mikka and I were shocked. We didn't expect it. Mikka gave me a look as if it was all my fault. He too strapped his skates on and told me that there was no place for arrogance and we will all fall apart this way. He too left on a bad note.

I couldn't sleep that night. I kept changing sides in my bed as I recalled how kids in the park wouldn't come up to me to play when I was little. As if it was not worth asking me, I was unfit for it. I couldn't run or hide or wasn't quick enough. That would get me sad. So I would just sit in my wheelchair looking around, observing other kids playing their own games, watching birds and trees, waiting for the sky to turn pink and orange in sunset. Until a little puppy came running up to me one day, sniffing my shoes and the wheels of my wheelchair. It didn't startle me just one bit. I was waiting for someone to come that close to me. His wagging tail showed his excitement to know me more, to be picked up by me. And then Mrs. Mistry walked up to me and put her little golden puppy into my arms. That was pure joy. He licked my face and just didn't want to be put down. This was our routine for the next few weeks. Mom and Mrs. Mistry would get busy in their hour long chit chats while Caesar would jump up onto my lap, snuggle up with me in the wheelchair and lick my hands asking me to rub his tummy and behind his ears. That attention from someone in the park was short-lived though. Mrs. Mistry had to go to

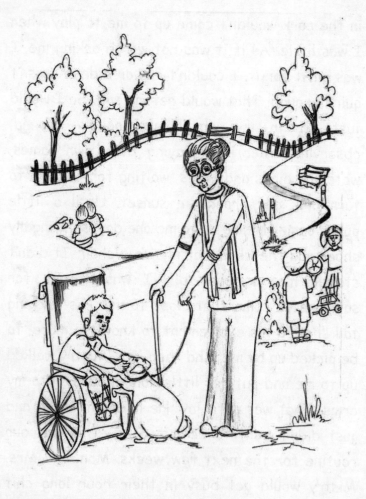

Bangalore to stay with her son, she was getting old and wanted some attention. And that meant, my new little friend, Caesar, was to go along too. The last day that we met in the park, Mrs.

Mistry and Mom clicked some pictures of us together. Mrs. Mistry even wheeled me behind Caesar who ran for a quick while and then looked back teasing us to catch him. It seemed like he knew we were playing the chase game.

🔧🔧🔧

Right before leaving for school the next day, I con-called Tara and Mikka.

"Umm... I am sorry guys. I am happy to take Caesar's case."

"Not before you both together solve the lecher's case," said Tara.

We could hear Mikka smiling at the other end.

🔧🔧🔧

Tara was not available in the meeting tonight as her cousins were coming over. But she had updated us on the plan which was to be executed tomorrow after school. The case was about the bus stop right outside Sarojini College for

Women where a lecher would sit and pass mean comments to college girls who boarded bus from there. Tara told us that he was given a lot of warnings from both the college staff and even the police, and he would disappear for a while, only to come back after a few weeks. And according to Tara's weird calculations, he was to return tomorrow again. Probably he was some kind of a maniac.

Mikka and I commenced our meeting while I jotted down the minutes of the meeting. No, that was not my idea. Tara told me to do so. She wanted to be updated later with the details. Of course, we told her that we could tell it all verbally, but she said this is not how organisations are run. I briefly thought of her perfect future plans of probably taking over her dad's Vasandani Industries.

Mikka raised a very good point of hiding our identity while working on the case so that people didn't recognise us, since it could risk our safety... mostly from our parents. And that could get us jacked big time. After brainstorming a few mask ideas and then coming to the conclusion that we couldn't create them overnight, we settled down at the idea of wearing helmets. We both had helmets at our home which were not in use.

"Perfect then. See you at the bus stop tomorrow at 1:15 PM."

I read online somewhere that Emma Watson never lagged behind in her studies while shooting for Harry Potter movies. That was the benchmark, I thought for myself. My superhero fame or disappearing lunchbox should not hamper my studies at school at any cost. Not even a small game of basketball of which I was not a part. I was a part of bigger things now. (The basketball part still hurt though.)

School got over and I wheeled out of the school... from the back gate. Deenu *kaka* waited for me at the front gate. I had only fifteen minutes to solve the case and reach back at the front gate before Deenu *kaka* suspected an emergency and walked inside the school in search of me. The school got over at 1 PM. But I had told Deenu *kaka* this morning that I will see him after school at 1:30 PM since I needed about thirty minutes to discuss about the upcoming science project with my partner. I also carried Dad's old silver helmet with me to school telling everyone at home that a 'needy friend' required it and since Dad now drove a car, he didn't need the helmet anymore, So we could give it to him. The 'friend' would return it back soon of course.

As I got further away from school, I put my helmet and super boosters on. I wondered if Mikka had reached the bus stop since it was a bit far from his school.

I neared the bus stop and saw that the bench was empty. There weren't any girls around as well. The location was completely deserted. Was the college closed today? Could Tara's calculations go wrong? What if the lecher also knew that the college was closed?

I decided to wait there for Mikka before wheeling back for school when my attention was taken by a few street dogs barking and growling at another dog much bigger than them. Indian street dogs never fail to amaze me. Their guts to chase just anyone or anything, especially in the night, are truly amazing. But this was daytime and I was getting bored. So I lazily took another look at the big dog that the street dogs were trying to scare. Scruffy golden coat, droopy eyes, collared neck - he seemed like a pet dog. For a brief moment, it struck me that it could be Mrs. Mistry's mysteriously disappeared dog, Caesar. My heart started racing. I wanted to confirm this. This dog was all grown up. In case he was Caesar, I wasn't even too sure if he would recognise me, though I'd heard that dogs, especially Labradors, have some real good memory. In a flash, it struck me to call out his name loudly.

"CAESAR!"

He instantly looked at me. It was Caesar. There was no doubt about it. I whistled at him to call him towards me. The other dogs too started taking steps towards me but retreated the very moment they saw a swarm of girls walking out of the gates of the college. Yes, the college gates had opened and the girls were walking out towards the bus stop. There was too much happening. I got scatter-brained. I didn't know what to do. To leap at Caesar? Or to save the girls from the road-side-Romeo? I quickly looked at the bus stop bench again just to make sure that Romeo wasn't there so that I could make the decision of going behind Caesar, who looked at me confused, his tail wagging slowly as if he was trying to decide, to come up to me or not to.

But it looked like my decision-making cells were on test today as I suddenly saw a man sitting on the bench at the bus stop. He was shabby looking, seemingly in his 20s and leered at the college girls, making them feel uncomfortable. This was the perfect moment that I call in Bankoo's Dictionary of Situations as 'DharmSankat'.

I slowly started wheeling towards the pestering man, adjusting my silver helmet, when I saw Mikka approaching from the other end. He came skating towards the bus stop on his rollerblades like fire. He wore a red helmet, and

I have no idea how he had fit it on his blue *patka* that showed from the sides. His hand was held high, and if my eyes were not mistaken, he held a hockey stick in that hand. Now that's what I call a dramatic entry! Can Sunny Deol beat that?

Mikka spotted me coming from the other end. And it seemed like he got more confident, or maybe, ferocious. And then things turned quite suddenly. Mikka looked at the creep, who had already noticed me. And then the creep looked at Mikka. Mikka shouted:

"Oyeee!!!! Teri tohhhh...[2]"

.

.

.

The creep ran away.

The girls ran away.

I ran away.

I need to explain why.

The creep ran away because he thought Mikka would actually hit him on his head and

---

2   *Let me teach you a lesson...*

since the creep was not wearing any helmet, well, he must run away.

The girls ran away because first they'd seen a weird little guy on wheelchair wearing helmet, and then suddenly they saw another little guy in helmet, skating insanely towards them. Fair enough.

I ran away because, well, Caesar was about to run away. And I knew Mikka was furious enough to scare the creep away by himself.

That evening Tara took us both on call.

"Who wears a helmet? Whose idea was it?" she barked.

We were quiet.

"Oh. Were you both trying to be smart? You were trying to be Batman or Spiderman."

We kept quiet.

"You scared the girls away. Everyone around is talking about the case. This is a breach of the confidentiality clause."

We didn't try to justify.

"Thank god they didn't see your faces."

That was because we were wearing helmets. But. We chose to keep our mouths shut.

"No helmet crap from now on," announced Tara.

"And... congrats on solving both the cases... with the sheer luck on your sides," she hung up.

"Sheer luck?! Did you hear that Mikka? No respect for bravery. No recognition. No appreciation."

He didn't hear much, he said.

THE VICIOUS VASOOLI BOSS

We didn't hold the meeting for two weeks and waited for the talks to die out. Tara finally called to give the good news that the lecher had stopped coming to the bus stop and was nowhere to be seen. So we planned to resume our midnight meeting.

The clock struck 11:59 PM.

I quietly wheeled out of the house towards the garage. I was so thrilled to meet Mikka and Tara after two long weeks. My heart made the sound of a basketball thumping hard on the court floor as I approached the garage gate...

Only to see the lock open.

THE DOOR WAS UNLOCKED.

I stopped dead in my tracks. There were sounds coming from inside. As my reflex forced my hand to instantly move on the pepper spray button (yes, imagine! I never thought of using it until now) I had this scary feeling that tonight the case I will be laying my hands on will not be that of Vasooli Boss, but theft in my own garage. That is if I manage to let the theft happen right now and runaway instead. But that won't happen. My middle name is Courage.

Bankoo Courage Bakshi incoming.

And I charged inside the garage... my hands ready to press the 'attack' buttons...

Only to find Tara and Mikka sitting on the stools, their pair of wheels parked against the wall.

"HOW? I DEMAND HOW... DID YOU GUYS ENTER?" I am sure I was loud enough as Mikka quickly turned to look at Tara.

Tara swung the keys around her index finger with that dangerous smile on her face, that which a TV soap vamp would give her venomous *saas*... or *bahu*... or whatever... I don't know. Mom had asked all her friends to strictly keep away from all this negative crap that came every hour on TV. They were more into Netflix series.

I checked my pocket again to find the original keys with me only. How did it happen then?

"I am not a thief, Bankoo. I guess you forgot. I am a tracker," remarked Tara.

"That's quite stalkerish Tara!" I commented.

"Yeah, I know. That one too." Tara laughed. Mikka tried to keep a poker face but couldn't hold it. So you can imagine, I couldn't do much.

I just joined them, and Tara shared with us the download about the case by writing the details on the blackboard Mom once used for teaching me and which was now dumped in the garage.

Bad Guy: Ronny *bhai* (famously known as Vasooli Boss)

Area: Maya Vihar, a residential place for the shopkeepers of the supermarket

Case: Forcibly collects *hafta* from the shopkeepers and tortures them

I interrupted Tara to ask how she got to know about the case since the market was not that near and she would never step out to a supermarket. Tara told us that she had overheard Raju *bhaiya* telling about this to his girlfriend, Pooja *didi*, over phone. 'Stalker', I

thought again. Mikka seemed to have read my

mind as we both exchanged secret looks and laughed in our heads.

"So what's the plan?" asked Mikka, all pepped up to beat the hell out of that Vasooli Boss.

Tara, being Tara, had done all the pre-work and had tracked Vasooli • Boss' past generations (and I am sure the ones to come). She started off.

"Every Friday evening, all the shopkeepers give their share of *hafta* to the old Head of the Supermarket, the owner of the biggest store, Mega Grocery Store. On Saturday, the Head, who is a poor old man, adds his own share and hands over all the money to the dreadful Vasooli Boss. As if that's not enough, the horrible guy creates a ruckus in his store, breaks things and picks some up to take along with him."

I could see from the corner of the eye that Mikka was already fuming up.

Tara continued, "I blackmailed Raju *bhaiya* just a slight bit to know more about him. After all, everyone has some weak point. Raju *bhaiya* told that Pooja *didi* was telling him just how horrible Vasooli Boss is and is not a loyal husband. He has an out of marriage affair with some evil woman, even worse than him, who lives quite near to his house." Tara paused to look at Mikka who was breathing heavily like a bull. For a moment I thought was it even a good idea to open my garage which was right next to my house, and let a bull inside.

Tara finally said the words we were waiting for as she took out a few photo printouts of a rough man with hideous stubble, holding close a woman that looked more like a seasoned criminal.

"So here's the plan. That's them, Vasooli Boss and his scary girlfriend secretly meeting at a place. We will stick out these print outs all around the place where he lives so that his wife, kids, and neighbours find out. I got to know from Raju *bhaiya* that the only person Vasooli Boss is scared of is his wife. She owns a house and ancestral property of her deceased father in a far off village and keeps asking Vasooli Boss to move some place nearer there so that she can take care of the place. But he doesn't want to,

because of his affair. And when she will get to know that he is having an illicit affair, she will eat him up alive. She will definitely drag him out from this area after all the humiliation. And he doesn't have the guts to leave her; she owns the property. And that should just work in our favour."

Women think so much, is all I could think of after listening to Tara's thought-over plan. And frankly, only a woman could have thought of that.

"I will put up the photo's huge posters outside his house and all around the area," said Tara.

"I will flatten up his car's tyres while he's at the Grocery Store collecting money so that he gets back home late. It'll buy you some time," said Mikka to Tara. He owned up some real badass work.

"I will keep Vasooli Boss and his goons occupied in the Supermarket. This will buy you some time to flatten the tyres." I was quite surprised with myself as I said this.

"Make sure no one sees you. Your skates are not super booster ready yet," said Tara.

"Let's make sure tomorrow is his last *hafta vasooli* day," I said invincibly.

We all high fived, and coordinated on timing and some last minute checks.

In the very end, I asked Tara to surrender the keys. She gave me an 'oh-really?' look and this logic:

"In case you doze off some night and miss our meeting? What will we do? I should have one duplicate key in that case. The meetings should go on."

I couldn't argue with her anymore, I was sleepy enough and it was a big day tomorrow. Dad once told his long-time college friend to never get into an argument with a woman. It can blast off in any direction... or she can blast off... I don't know which one I had heard him saying.

So as we winded up, I proposed to Mikka and Tara that probably instead of a pepper spray, they could invent some *Mirchi* Bombs to fit into Turbo maybe. Tara asked me to submit a written application for the same with some valid reasons in support, and probably then they'll consider the request. She had mounted on her uber cool and super-fast Segway by now.

I opened my mouth to again argue with Tara, but Mikka gave me a secret look that it might not be a good idea right now. As Tara looked at Mikka, he instantly looked down to put on his skates.

I was damn sleepy by now. And equally excited for tomorrow. I had no idea how I would stop the horrible Vasooli Boss from collecting *hafta*, or keeping him occupied until Tara put up posters of his doomed fate.

BUN MASKA TIME

Saturday, 11 AM: "Deenu *kaka*, I don't want to have breakfast."

"Why? Have milk at least."

"No, not even milk."

"Why are you acting so weird since morning?"

How could I explain Deenu *kaka* that it was a very important case and that I was nervous, and that by feeding me, he would actually be feeding the butterflies in my stomach and I am sure they didn't want to have anything either.

"I had a sleepless night."

"Of course. That's because you were watching Golmaal. I saw the cover of the CD on the table."

"Please drop me at Tara's place Deenu *kaka*. She is holding a brunch at her place. Mom knows about it." I royally ignored his comment. Someone explain to him that watching the movie was for strictly research purposes.

"Yes, *didiji* told me. We are leaving for her house in two minutes. Let me just clean the table. And keep the CD in its place before *didiji* gets to know of your late night moves." For a moment there my heart stopped as I checked Deenu *kaka*'s facial expressions for any signs of his knowing of our secret meetings at the garage. But then I remembered how Deenu *kaka* snored like a beast and no one, not even Dad could wake him up after 11 PM for any big small requests. Unless there was an earthquake, and we can just hope he would get up at least then to save himself.

But right now, I had to go save those poor shopkeepers.

Tara and I escaped from her house's hardly-ever-used backdoor, the existence of which, I am sure even Vasandani uncle had long forgotten. I put Turbo on gear five and zoomed off, while Tara wheeled her Segway in the other direction. Mikka had already left for the market directly from his house.

I reached Mega Grocery Store just before 12 PM. I was having some problems entering the store because the platform was a bit raised but the old uncle, who seemed to be the store owner, came over and tilted Turbo a bit. I thanked him and ventured into the store on a relatively empty aisle, pretending to check out burger buns. I had hardly whiled away for five minutes, mostly thinking of how awesome was it riding Turbo all by myself at such a cool speed, and how I had full control over all the functions now... when some loud voices at the counter startled me. I silently wheeled towards the counter trying to hide myself along the aisle. This is what I saw.

A muscular man of medium height and a stubbled face, eyes covered with a funny pair of round glares, ears pierced, neck flaunting chains of gold, and almost every finger of his hand ringed. He sure as hell was the infamous Vasooli Boss. Just when I thought 'typical', I happened

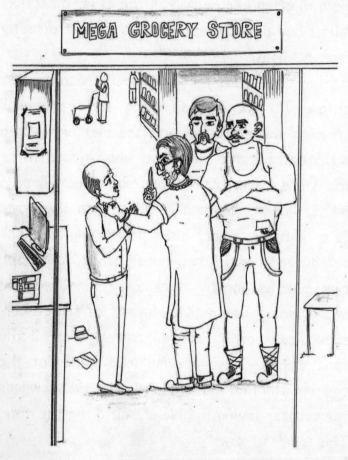

to checkout Vasooli Boss' attire – he was wearing a black kurta and a blue pair of denims. Ha! Perfect timing.

I quickly started wheeling towards the counter. The owner, Vasooli Boss and his two goons got interrupted and looked at me. I instantly grabbed a pen and paper lying on the counter and wheeled further towards Vasooli. Stretching out my hand that held the paper and pen towards Vasooli, I jabbered:

"Vasooli Boss, Can I get your autograph?"

"What?" blurted Vasooli.

The goons exchanged looks. Owner uncle looked puzzled. Vasooli Boss too looked at the owner uncle for a second.

"Yes Boss, *your* autograph. I am a big fan of yours. You totally look like Arshad Warsi in that movie, *Munna Bhai M.B.B.S.*" I said enthusiastically.

"You mean Circuit," said one of the goons, guffawing at his own remark. The other one covered his giggles with his muscular arms.

"Ae! Shut up," slammed Vasooli Boss at both of them.

He turned towards me, a bit starry eyed.

"Umm... Do I?"

The fish had got hooked.

"Yes, of course Boss. Totally. You have that personality, Vasooli Boss. You have that style! I am telling you. You should be working in movies. Why are you wasting your time here?" I was quite impressed with my flattery skills.

And Vasooli Boss had totally bought it. He gave a ridiculous shy smile, as the gap in his mouth from the broken tooth showed. He seemed to be in the mood to grab some more flattery. So I continued the *maska*...

"Exact smile Vasooli Boss. Waah! You have a killer smile."

From the corner of my eye, I caught a glimpse of owner uncle flinching at the word 'killer'. I thought of explaining him my slang later.

The smile had changed into a loud laughter now, and I must say a really silly one. It sounded like a donkey braying. And the sight of his gapped teeth with little black holes in between was not a very nice one. Now I know what Mom means when she keeps reminding me of brushing my teeth every night.

"Did you guys listen to that? Hee..haww..heehee..haww... I knew it. I am no less than a star. Ae boy! Where is that paper? Let me sign it. And listen you, boy. Though I don't see you doing much in the future with that... (he pointed to Turbo) ...but you can come to me maybe, I will find something for you," said the dumb-head Vasooli Boss.

I felt like wheeling back towards the very end of the aisle, putting the Turbo on super booster mode and give a flying punch into that idiot's face but calmed myself to faking a smile on my face that was red by now.

Vasooli Boss signed the paper harshly, almost scratching it off, and threw it on the counter for me to pick it up. He snatched the money that was still there in the owner uncle's hand. Owner uncle looked at me as if he couldn't believe I could turn up that insane. I wish I could tell him the entire plan but our pact didn't allow me to do that.

As Vasooli Boss and his stupid muscle men rushed towards their car which by now would have been flat-tyred by Mikka, I started wheeling out of the Store. I looked back once more to see owner uncle's face and he still threw a half angry half puzzled look.

"Uncle, this is the last time you've seen Vasooli Boss and his men. No need to collect money from next week onward."

I quickly wheeled away and disappeared on my Turbo.

THE THREE COMMANDMENTS OF MIKKA'S GARAGE

Surely Mikka had done his job and I am sure no one had seen him. I hid myself behind a car and watched their moves. Vasooli Boss and his goons had found their car's flatten tyre. They looked here and there, swearing and hitting the tyre of their Scorpio. And then one of the goons asked the other for the Stepney.

Oh heck! Why didn't we think of this part? They would simply change the tyre and go. As the other goon looked under the Scorpio, he started acting like he had got a fit. I tried looking under the car and understood what had happened. The Stepney was missing.

When I would have been busy preparing for my role, someone had already thought through his. And that was Mikka, the fantastic car freak! I saw Mikka entering the scene.

"What happened sir? Can I help you?" said Mikka, casually walking towards Vasooli Boss.

I am sure by now the shopkeepers were thinking that something's gone wrong with the kids around this place. Daring to collect autographs or casually ask questions from Vasooli Boss, the mad *Hafta* Collector of the area. They stood outside their shops not believing their eyes.

"*Achhaa*?! Now *you* will help me? You chump! It's a flat tyre. And the Stepney is stolen too. Why don't you fix that for me boy? I swear I am going to kill that scoundrel who has dared doing this to me." Vasooli Boss had fumed up and trembled as he spoke.

"Sir, my garage is just nearby, and spare tyres and other parts are available. I can definitely help you with this." Mikka looked into Vasooli's eye as he said this. Almost like he was challenging him.

Vasooli Boss had nothing to say, so he signalled the goons and they all left for Mikka's garage. Mikka showed them the way. The plan was going well.

"Sir, this is the form that you need to sign," said Mikka, handing over a form to Vasooli Boss before entering his garage.

"Form?! What form?" growled Vasooli Boss.

"Sir, a few rules of the garage. One: only you can enter the garage, and not your fellow men, since it's *your* car. Two: you cannot carry a mobile phone inside. I'll tell you the third rule, if there is any requirement sir, as of now, I don't see any."

"What?! What kind of rules are these? Which garage keeps them?" Vasooli Boss looked both funny and angry opening his mouth with grit gapped teeth showing.

"We do sir. Rule one is for safety purposes. And the second rule is to avoid distraction. If our workers get distracted by the funny or aggressive videos that you might watch whiling away your time, they will not be able to work, sir. Please cooperate. Any way this is lunch time and we are going out of our way to help you. There is no other garage nearby." Mikka said matter-of-factly. He was rude without even trying.

Strangely, Vasooli Boss felt helpless and had surrendered by now, or was actually tired. He snatched the form and signed it.

"Just get it over with. I am hungry, I have to leave." He slammed the form against Mikka's chest, who got a bit shaken by the jolt but didn't let it come on his face.

This was Mikka's plan. Vasooli Boss wouldn't be much of a boss without the two goons, and would not create a ruckus inside the garage just by himself. Such men are weak inside when left alone. And the 'no cell phone' rule was to save Vasooli Boss himself from his wife, until the time he reached home at least. He didn't want the giant fight to be on phone inside his garage already, now that his wife would have found out about his affair by now.

Mikka's mechanics did what was to be done in less than forty minutes and Vasooli Boss was free to go. They zoomed away as Vasooli Boss' doomed fate waited for him to arrive at home. We all reached Tara's place by 2 PM according to our plan. Tara was laughing madly as she rode her Segway towards the back gate, where I had been waiting and was joined by Mikka just a while ago.

"What happened Tara?" Mikka and I asked desperately.

"Dude. You both should have seen his wife's reaction. Poor woman! She dropped dead in the middle of the road. Her face changed a hundred colours as she called names to Vasooli, who wasn't even there yet. The entire neighbourhood collected outside her house as she threw television, microwave and don't know what all out of her house. I wish I could see her giving a chokeslam to Vasooli. I am sure he will be seen nowhere after this gets over," told Tara, all content.

"How will we be sure that Vasooli and his goons will not be turning up at the Supermarket next week?" I asked.

"You don't have to worry about that. The news will be confirmed by tomorrow afternoon. My local Newswala will let me know," said Tara, again with that vicious smile.

"Local *Newswala* who?" Mikka and I looked at Tara curiously.

"Chill. I'll call you guys tomorrow afternoon to tell the confirmed news. Now you must leave for your home Mikka. And Bankoo, let's get inside before Deenu *kaka* knocks at the door again."

"How do you know that he had knocked before?" I asked, staring wide-eyed at Tara.

"Twice," she confirmed.

"How do you know?" I begged.

"Chill. Why do you guys ask so many questions!" and she again threw that wicked smile.

"Guess what Tara? You and this word 'chill' don't go well together." I snapped.

Mikka chuckled. Tara gave me a look.

We all said goodbye to each other, and reached our houses, acting like nothing had happened. All we knew was that the adventures had begun. Our life was on a roll.

Tara took Mikka and me on a conference call at dot 2 PM the next day.

"Mission accomplished!"

ENCOUNTER WITH JAGGA AND KALIA

I was still unable to make friends at school. Everyone had started to stare at me a bit less though. But the P.T. period and lunchbox dilemma was pretty much the same. Somehow P.T. period was the only period when no one stared at me. They didn't have the time to.

I promised myself I'll ask Mom proactively to give me food in a Haldiram box. The thought of chaining that Haldiram box with my schoolbag also came to my mind. But then I dropped the idea out of the fear of again grabbing unnecessary attention from everyone at school.

But this was the day that was to be marked as life-changing in my future biography. I returned back home, changed my uniform, had my lunch, did my homework, gave a phone call to

Mikka and Tara, and then dozed off for a quick nap. It seemed like an ordinary day.

It was also a do-one-independent-task day, and I had to finally go buy some vegetables from the local market on the next street. I had decided to make the evening a bit exciting by trying the automation of the wheelchair, now that I was officially all by myself.

Zip Zap Zooooom!!

Alright no.

Zip zap zip zap zip zap zap! That's how life was at gear one on Turbo. Decent.

All I know was it was worth it.

The people in the market had never seen me before, unlike the other regular customers and so everyone stared at me... and Turbo.

Now that I was grabbing so much attention, I felt like wheeling towards the Chowk, in the heart of the market, with a mike in my hand and announce, 'Hello people, I'm Bankoo and this is Turbo. We are here to save the World.'

Turbo stumbled a bit over a stone. I guess it didn't like the idea much.

I adjusted myself on Turbo and took out the list of vegetables that Mom had given me for buying.

1. Tamatar[3]   1kg
2. Onions   1kg
3. Potatoes   1kg
4. Beans   1 bundle
5. Carrots   1kg
6. Cauliflower 1 medium sized

I wonder when she wrote everything in English, what was the deal with 'Tamatar'.

Anyway, with years I had realised, on a few things you should never question the lady of the house. It can get dangerous, you know. No, I didn't. This piece of advice came from Dad's survival kit.

I thought of using a reasonable idea from my own survival kit. To avoid the constant stares, I could ideally start from the very end of the market and then slowly and gradually enter towards the popular Chowk, where the crowd was thickest. Yeah, that would work well.

---

3   Tomatoes

While reaching the end of the market, I easily shifted from gear one to gear two. The road was not at all crowded with people. I was about to reach the last hawker who had only one customer and was looking at me with high hopes. Less of curiosity and more of hope in his eyes, I could do with that combination of stare. As I was about to reach that hawker, my chair stumbled again, and this time I guess I had run over on someone's foot. Yikes!

I looked back to see a lady crying, panting and trying to run, shouting '*Chor! Chor! Pakdo! Pakdo!*[4]'. I looked in the same direction as she was running and saw two people on the bike driving away with the lady's bag in their hand.

My hands instantly went on the red button.

Woooooooshh... Zaaaapppp!!!

Turbo and I went dashing.

I quickly fastened my seat belt as I raced in the direction of those thieves.

---

4   *Thief! Thief! Catch him! Catch him!*

Turbo and I caught up with their bike soon. Was I dreaming?

Both of them looked at me with their jaws dropped. I had no time to waste.

I quickly tapped the left armrest hard and out popped the can full of nails. I tilted the mouth of the can towards the bikers while it shot out nails. It somehow missed their face, but the fallen nails didn't miss the bike's back tyre. The bike slipped, and the muggers crashed. It was the right time to snatch back that aunty's bag while they were still in shock.

Screeeeeeech!!!

I pulled the breaks and wheeled on gear one towards the thief who held the bag loosely. He was still managing to get up. I took the opportunity and snatched the bag, quickly wore it cross bodied, pushed the lever straight to gear four, and dashed away. The thief somehow tried to grab my arm, but Turbo had picked up speed by then.

Phew! That was close.

I reached back at the same spot and handed over the bag to aunty who had informed the police by now. She thanked me and gave a hundred blessings, and so did the other people around.

What satisfaction when you give someone happiness. And a bag full of... money?! I guess.

I returned back home all happy and content with that accomplished feeling. Mom opened the door, and guess what?

I'm sure you would have forgotten it too... the vegetables.

"Where are the vegetables?" demanded Mom, looking at me with those piercing eyes.

"Oh heck. I forgot!"

"How could you forget it?" yelled Mom. "What did you go to the market for?" she growled.

"To save the world." My lips blurted.

Damn! That's not how I should have said it.

I had almost perished under Mom's laser beam gaze by now when police intervened... and saved me.

They had probably got to know the entire story from that aunty and the market vendor witnesses and told my mother about the whole episode. Mom was too shocked and was staring at my wheelchair with her eyes almost popped out. The laser beam had vanished though.

The police wanted a sketch of both the snatchers. I helped them with the details of how exactly they looked. After the sketch was complete, both the snatchers were recognised as Jagga and Kalia, well-known goons whom the police was after.

Mom was frozen already and wanted some time to get herself back. She waited for Dad to come. I thought it was a good idea since boys are good at handling boy stuff.

Meanwhile, I called Mikka and Tara to tell them all that had happened. I also told Tara that I didn't really need the pepper spray, shooting nails were enough. But Tara virtually slapped me and so Mikka had to change the topic.

I thought this was more than enough for me to own a Wikipedia page, but wait till you see what came next.

STALKER TARA SCREWS IT UP

My Haldiram tiffin box got stolen.

I wondered if my school belonged to hell.

Model Public School

Wretched Road Number 13

Dwell In Hell – 666

Netherworld

I thought of asking Mom to pack me two lunchboxes from now on, one for that invisible hungry pig and the other for me, this poor soul. But Mom called me a careless soul.

It takes some specific combination of cells in your body to find out negative from the most positive of the situations. And my Mom's body was full of those cells.

She still managed to give me a lecture on how I should have not shown those stunts and waited with aunty for the police to arrive and for them to take the matter in their hands. Dad gave me silent support by remaining silent on the issue.

They both decided to not discuss about this event with anyone and suggested me to not Turbo around since they were not used to handling any extra attention. The weird stares at me were already so much for them.

I returned back home from school super hungry and was hunting for some biscuits while Deenu *kaka* laid the food on the table when the phone rang.

It was Tara.

"Come home now. I have to show you something."

From her voice, I had already got the idea that she was up to something major.

"Alright, after lunch and nap," I answered. The smell of food was much more tantalizing than whatever Tara had to flaunt. I didn't even wait to say her goodbye and dropped the phone to rush to the dining table.

Gobble... Guzzle... Hog... Hogged

Burp!

Nap time.

* * *

The landline showed 5 missed calls, all from Tara.

I quickly freshened up. Mom had arrived from office by now. I told her I'll make a quick visit to Tara's and be back soon.

"Hold your horses Bankoo, Deenu *kaka* will go with you," Mom commanded.

"I hope you remember what we discussed," she hissed.

"Of course, Mom."

* * *

Tara thanked Deenu *kaka* as soon as we reached, and wheeled me into her roomatory.

"Guess what I did yesterday Bankoo?" beamed Tara.

"Umm... Created your own Jarvis?" I joked.

"Duh! No. You got to see this for yourself!" said Tara as she turned towards her Apple desktop.

As I looked onto the screen, I saw flowing frequency waves on the left corner and different locations blinking on a map on the right.

What map was it? Hold on a minute. It was our town's map. What was this girl up to again?!

I just looked at her with my eyes wide open.

Tara started. "With these codes, I can intercept the calls that come to our town's police. That way, we can pick and solve the simple cases like the one you tackled in the vegetable market the other day. The police will have no clue about the calls as they'll directly reach us only. Mikka, you and I will quarantine the town from bugs - I mean burglars," she said ambitiously.

I gasped. I gulped. I choked.

"ARE YOU OUT OF YOUR MIND?!! What have you been thinking? You think what you did is cool? It's a crime, Tara. You're messing up with the town's system and the police. Do you even realise how bad it can end up? This is completely careless of you. Remove this coding and the system hack right away, before we get into a bigger trouble!" I exploded at Tara.

Bleep... Bleep... Bleep...

Suddenly the speakers attached to the desktop hooted.

A voice followed. 'Hello... this is Khabri. I saw two kids being kidnapped by two men in a van numbered DH 4S AD 6666 near Jawahar Lane, I repeat it was Omni van number DH 4S AD 6666.'

Beeeeeeeeeeeep.

Tara and I looked at each other in horror. We were doomed.

"Was this an intercepted call?" I asked horrified.

"Yes", Tara answered with a sorry face.

"We don't have much time. I need to think of something quick. If the police get to know about this, our parents will be informed, or worst case, we will get punished. Most importantly, this information needs to reach the police as soon as possible. It's a matter of someone's life. And Tara, stop the coding right now, you are not doing this again. Ever."

Tara did as told.

By the time an idea had clicked me.

"I know Commissioner Uncle's house, it's nearby. I'm going there to tell him everything that just happened and give him the important information that Khabri gave. I'll apologise on our behalf too and let's see what happens." As I said this, I put on my seat belt and started for the main door. Tara apologised and asked me to take care of myself while she followed my track on the GPS.

She was born to be a techie I guess, she just didn't know where to stop.

I dashed for Commissioner Uncle's house gear by gear. The signal blinked and showed low battery. I sometimes had to appreciate God's timing.

The house's guards were kind enough to quickly take me to Commissioner Uncle, and he was the most patient listener. I realised he was kind too. He accepted the apologies and told that we should draw a line and not play with the systems. He had already called the control room, passed on the information and gave them an action plan by the time.

While Commissioner Uncle got busy handling the situation with other officers, it was time for me to leave. I explained the guard that I could really go by myself the way I had come and they needn't worry. I quickly wheeled towards home as it was getting dark and Mom might end up bursting at me again.

Ten minutes had already passed, and I was ten more minutes away from home when a car swooshed by on the empty road. It got me thinking that I should have a headlight on my Turbo too, it would be helpful in the night.

Just then that same car, which happened to be an Omni van, came driving back in reverse direction and stopped right next to me. Not a good feeling.

The driver seemed to peep out of the window to look at me. Not a good feeling at all.

I looked at the driver and recognised his face. It was Jagga, the purse snatcher. I tried putting Turbo on fifth gear, but it was too late now. Another man came out from the back seat and leapt towards me. He was no other than Kalia. I quickly pressed the nail can button, but nothing came out. Damn! It was not refilled after the vegetable market incident. Kalia was face to face with me and had grabbed my arm when I managed to press the other can's button. Out popped the pepper spray, shooting right into his eyes. He screamed and howled in pain. I pushed the button to kick off the super boosters, but the battery had died. I manually started to wheel off but knew my fate. Jagga got down from the car and grabbed me. He pushed me into the car and locked me inside.

"Aaaaargh! My eyes are burning Jagga. I will not spare this boy. Take his wheelchair too, I will break both of them and dump them somewhere far," said Kalia violently. Jagga did as was told. He threw Turbo in the back *dikki*.

After what would have been a twenty minute drive, criminal Jagga pulled me out of the van and dragged me away like some luggage. Kalia could not open his eyes and was still in pain. He tried to catch up with Jagga holding his shirt from behind.

I happened to look at the car as I was being dragged away.

It was that same Omni van with the number plate DH 4S AD 6666.

I felt like a vegetable.

THE DEADLY KIDNAPPING

The place looked like some kind of an old warehouse no longer in use. The lights were fairly dim, and there wasn't much visible to the eyes.

Jagga threw me on the floor and both left to get water for furious Kalia's burning eyes.

I was trying to get myself together when I heard sobs coming from a corner.

"Who is it?" My voice echoed.

The sobs continued. I heard some rustling from the same direction.

"Who's it in that corner?" I asked with a shivering voice.

I heard slow footsteps and then saw two boys walking towards me, the taller one was holding the hand of the other boy who sobbed.

As they came closer, their faces showed up. The taller one, a well-built boy, was none other than Cheap Joydeep, the dude from our school, the captain of the basketball team. The other boy seemed to be his younger brother, and they looked quite similar.

So they were the two boys who had got kidnapped? We were three now.

"You are kidnapped too?" Cheap Joydeep asked me. "Why did they kidnap you?"

"To take revenge on me." I answered, "And what are they getting from you?"

"Money." said Cheap Joydeep, "Our father is in Dubai on a business trip. These kidnappers said they'll beat us up and send our pictures to dad and blackmail him." Shivers ran down my spine.

"But revenge from you? What have you done?" he continued to ask.

"I saved an aunty's bag from being snatched by them a few days back."

Both the brothers looked at me.

"She's our mom." The younger boy spoke.

He slowly walked towards me and said, "*Bhaiya*, can you save us too? Can you take us on your wheelchair? I don't want to be here." He started crying.

For the first time in my life, I was being looked up to by someone, and I was in such a helpless state.

"I'm sorry brother, but I'm helpless. My wheelchair's battery was dying when they found me. I couldn't even wheel away. I don't even have my crutches with me." My voice choked as I said this. I tried to cover my face with my hands, trying to recollect myself.

Both of them came forward and helped me get up. They slowly took me to a corner so that I could take the support of the wall. Joydeep looked here and there in the dim room as his eyes searched for something. He quickly dashed to grab two rods from somewhere and handed them to me. I tried my grip on them, they were quite fitting, and I could stand with their support. For a while at least.

As this happened, I took another view of the place, this time my mind was clearer. There were rods, big tins of oil and grease and some tool junk lying here and there. I looked at not-so-cheap Joydeep. He was observing me and somehow understood what I had on my mind.

"No chance Bankoo. We are only kids. We cannot fight them. I've seen knives in their hands," said Joydeep. I wondered how he knew my name.

"You may be right, we are just kids. But those goons are weak. One of them is blinded by the pepper spray that I used on him. And the police are on the way. We can dodge them by the time police comes to our rescue." I explained.

"How do you know the police are on the way?" Joydeep asked. He looked hopeful suddenly.

"I'll tell you later. We don't have time for this. The kidnappers must be coming back any moment now. Let's just use whatever tools are there in this place, and fight for our lives." As I said this, I myself had no idea what would I do.

"Oh ho! Look who's that helpless loser?"

The two nasty scoundrels were back.

Kalia still had his eyes red and was constantly rubbing them, trying to see. His red eyes made him look even more beastly.

"You cripple, you thought you could get away from us. This is all because of you. You didn't let us snatch that bag full of money. And so we had to kidnap these two rats to get the money out from their father. And we know he will not give us a single penny till we break his sons' bones and send to him for dinner." As Jagga said this he raised his hand to hit Joydeep hard.

Whack!

I managed to hit Jagga with my new found rod in his abdomen. He held his stomach and cried in pain. I was generally not a violent person, and this move got me by surprise. The red eyed Kalia took two steps back in shock. This was the time.

I looked at Joydeep and shouted, "you are a basketball champ right? So tall and such well-built. Why don't you show us some dribbling skills here?"

Joydeep looked at the red-eyed Kalia who had got cold feet.

"Joydeep, come on! If I can do it, so can you."

Smack!

Joydeep let out a tight slap on the red-eyed monster.

"How dare you call us a rat? Let me tell who the rat is," said Joydeep and attacked Kalia's face with more and more slaps, much tighter than Mrs. Reddy's.

"Argghhhh..."

Hit Jagga was recovering by now, he held his knife and leapt at me in complete rage.

Thudaam!

Off he went on the floor, his head spinning as he went in shock.

What just happened?

I saw Joydeep's brother chuckle. He had rolled a tin full of oil, and the goon had hit the floor as soon as he put his foot on it.

Kalia's face, just like his eyes, had turned red. He pushed away Joydeep and took out lighter from his pocket.

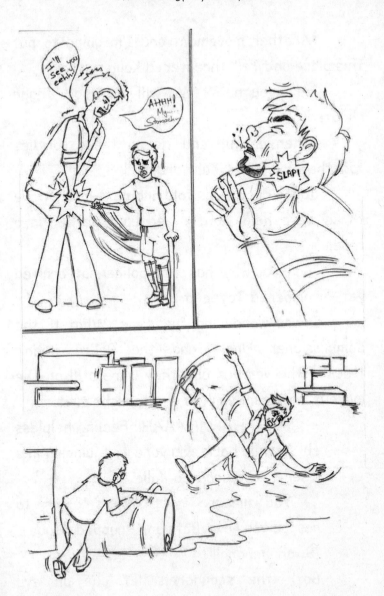

"Another movement and I'm going to put this place on fire," threatened Kalia.

"Are you nuts? We will die too." Jagga shouted.

"Then get up and tie up these rowdies together you idiot," Kalia ordered.

Jagga did as was told and next moment we three were held tightly tied up together in a rope.

"Bankoo, why has the police not arrived yet?" whispered Joydeep.

I was wondering the same. What if the Commissioner Uncle and the Police hadn't tracked the van yet and they were still on the lookout. My heart sank at the thought of it.

"HAHAHAHAHAAAH!! Feeling helpless eh! A while back everyone was jumping like a superhero!" roared Kalia.

"You meagre rats! Who's going to rescue you now? Batman?' snapped Jagga. "Bwahahahaha!!!"

Both the scoundrels let out an evil laughter.

"Let's teach them a lesson." Kalia said with burning eyes.

CRRASHHHH...!!!!

THUDD!!

Someone broke the glass window and entered the place.

Everyone was stunned and looked in the direction from where the voice came. We saw a vague figure of someone holding a rod high up in his hands and running towards us.

Running? No. Skating!

The figure came closer and closer.

Oh boy! It was MIKKA!!

How on Earth did he reach this place?

And it wasn't a rod in his hand, it was a cricket bat.

"*Bole Sonihaaaaaal......*"

Why was he always that dramatic?

Jagga and Kalia had a confused look on their faces. But then they got ready with the knives in their hand.

"Stop right there otherwise we will kill you!" threatened Jagga.

Mikka kept skating.

"I'm telling you, if you don't stop, we are going to finish you," threatened Kalia.

Mikka didn't stop.

"This boy is so daring. Who is he?" said Joydeep, staring at him in shock.

"He is my best friend, Mikka. And he is hard of hearing!" I gulped in fear. He wasn't wearing his hearing aid.

Jagga warned again, "*O sardarji*, if you don't stop right now, we will staaaaaabbbb...."

WHACKKK!!!

"*Satsriaaakaaaaal!*"

Mikka hit Jagga's face hard with his bat. Jagga passed out right away.

Kalia lifted the hand in which he held the knife and pounced towards Mikka...

BOOM!!!

Kalia fell on the floor howling in pain. He was shot with a bullet in his leg.

The police had arrived.

Mikka and the police freed us and checked if we were fine. Both Jagga and Kalia were arrested and taken into police custody.

We were taken out from the warehouse. Mom-Dad were waiting outside, and so were Joydeep's parents. They ran towards us and hugged us. Tara was there too, she handed over my crutches. Mom couldn't stop crying. I told her I was fine. Joydeep told everything to the

Police, and they appreciated the three of us for our courage and presence of mind. Everyone laughed and patted Mikka too. Dad handed over Mikka's hearing aid which he had dropped in Dad's car.

I saw the Commissioner Uncle talking to Tara and shaking hands with her. I think I was missing on something here.

Finally, Mom Dad made me sit in the car. Tara and Mikka joined too. Turbo was already tied up to the roof of our car. It was rescued from the van of death.

"How did the Police find us?" I shot the question. I desperately wanted to know.

Dad started, "Through Tara's GPS system. When she saw that your wheelchair had abruptly stopped somewhere in the middle of the road, and after a few minutes it started off in the opposite direction at a relatively high speed, Tara called Mikka. She checked with him on the speed of the super boosters. But your wheelchair seemed to be moving at a much higher speed which meant that your wheelchair and probably you as well were in some other moving vehicle. So both Mikka and Tara called the Police and reached home to tell us everything about your visit to the Commissioner. We quickly reached the spot where you had stopped and found the pepper spray bottle. Tara told it was hers and highlighted that probably you were in some deep trouble. The Police and Tara followed the GPS system, and we managed to reach on this spot where the van was found."

"But Turbo's battery had already died. How could it be tracked?" I pointed out.

"The GPS system can run on backup for 2 hours," Tara answered.

"Tara was very quick to act." Mom said as she kissed Tara.

"Thanks Tara! And now I understand why Commissioner Uncle was shaking hands with you." I mentioned.

"Oh that. No no, he was asking me if I could be a part of his special secret techie team sometime later." Said Tara.

"Whaaat? Wow!" That was the only noise I could make.

I looked at Mikka and asked him, "what's with the bat and skates?"

"Oh *yaar*. I had lied to papaji that I'm going to the garage to mend the wheels of my skates, but I was going to play cricket with my friends. Tara came to pick me up at the park itself to go to your place." He started guffawing.

"By god, this was my best sixer!"

Everyone laughed.

THE TURBO GANG

The Commissioner Uncle told us we are all special and deserved a special mention. However, Tara, in her fit of modesty, requested him to not mention our names to any newspapers or so. She said we all were to keep this a secret so that we could keep helping the city in our own small ways. And we didn't need any limelight.

I told Tara that she had ruined my superhero career because I could work much better under the limelight. But she said life would get really complex that way. I thought of Spiderman's life for a moment and then chucked the idea for some time.

But my school life got somewhat cool.

Everyone still stared at me including Joydeep. But it was more like how Gryffidors would look at Harry Potter when he would return from the Quidditch match.

I enjoyed the attention until it was P.T. period again. So I wheeled to the side of the court already waiting for it to get over.

"Bankoo... Bankoooo!" Joydeep called me.

He walked up to me and asked:

"Will you be a part of our basketball team?"

My jaws dropped, mouth opened wide only to say nothing.

"I consider it a yes then," he smiled and wheeled me into the court.

This was better than anything that I could have wished for. I was a part of the Basketball Team! I felt butterflies in my stomach.

We were so excited, Joydeep and I ended up playing basketball during the lunch break too.

Rest of the periods passed by smoothly, school ended and Deenu *kaka* wheeled me home. I was still kept on the pact by parents that I would not use Turbo on gears and super boosters until and unless really required. I didn't mind that as long as I was having secret fun in the garage every night.

Evening came, and so did Mom, Tara, and Mikka. Mom had called them for evening snacks. We ate, laughed and chit chatted. I told them that I was a part of the Basketball team now and we played during lunchtime too.

And then it happened.

"Bankoo, if you kept playing during the lunchtime, you wouldn't have eaten your lunch. Take out your lunchbox before it soils your schoolbag," suggested Mom.

You would have got to know by now the deep emotional connection between mothers and lunchboxes.

I agreed and fetched my schoolbag.

No lunchbox!

Front pocket – no lunchbox.

Side pockets – not there.

Main zip – not there either.

I was robbed off my lunchbox again. Who would do that now? Who does that to Harry Potter?! I mean, Bankoo, the Turbo Rider!

Mom's expressions changed, and the forehead started wrinkling up. Not a good sign.

I saw Mikka removing his hearing aid. Such an escapist.

I quickly looked at Tara and asked, "Tara, can you fit GPS into my next lunchbox?"

"Actually I can," she said, as they all burst into laughter.

Night came, and we met at my garage for our meeting.

We were all excited to meet tonight. It was the night of celebration and Mikka somehow couldn't stop grinning. We knew he was longing to tell us something. So before Mikka could start, Tara stood up with the red diary in her hand, which officially spelled 'RULE BOOK' now, and announced:

"Guys, I'm proud of you. You've been extraordinary. And Bankoo, you were heroic to fight back without Turbo. That needs courage. It was huge."

This was the moment I thought I should request her to open my Wikipedia page, but Tara continued, "I officially announce the titles 'Turbo Rider' to Bankoo, 'Inventor' to Mikka, and 'Tracker' to myself. We promise to be together through thick and thin and to save the city with whatever we can. We will put our skills to use and help the people, making this world a safer place."

"Wow. This still feels like a dream." I said.

"The dream is yet to come true Bankoo," said Mikka. This time he held a Tara-like smile.

"What do you mean?" asked Tara.

Mikka looked at Tara and then at me, "Bankoo, I have built something for you."

Tara and I looked puzzled.

"TURBO Version 2 in the making," he let out the words under his breath.

Tara let out a squeak and quickly covered her mouth. My jaws dropped. Mikka nodded excitedly.

"My cousin was coming back from the U.S., so I asked him to get some real badass stuff, and you have no idea what I've been able to create out of it," Mikka said effusively.

My mind was blown. I was thrilled beyond belief.

Tara sprang up and hugged us both.

"I think this is going to be so much fun." she jumped in excitement.

"Oh yes, so much fun." I finally found my voice.

"Our gang should have a name," suggested Mikka.

"Whizz Kids maybe?" said Tara.

"Umm... Nope. The Turbo Gang!" I announced.

We were ready for our next mission.

THE END

And then came a mysterious letter...

From the SECRET SOCIETY OF ABILITIES!!

Contest Alert!
#WHATSYOURMUTATION

We believe every kid has a mutation; any kid can have super powers.

What is your mutation? What can you do differently to bring a small change around you?

Grab your pen and fill your answer here:

_____

_____

_____

_____

_____

_____

_____

_____

Take a photo of this page and send it to the Author at rushati.ghosh@gmail.com

Best entry will win a SURPRISE GIFT, and also a CHANCE to be a CHARACTER in the next book.

Terms & Conditions:

1. Your participation is only valid if you have sent a photo of this page filled with your answer.

2. You have to present the book and this page with the originally written answer to claim the win.